# THE KIRKLYN HORROR

J. M. DeSantis

Also by J. M. DeSantis
*Robert Phillips*


Children's Book
*Ghosts Are People Too*


Comics
*Chadhiyana* (series)
*Gentleman Cthulhu* (series, comic strip)
*The Tainted Ones*


Memoir, Writing, & Art Collection
*J. M. DeSantis: The First Ten Years*

# the Kirklyn Horror

J. M. DeSantis

Dark Fire Press
New Jersey, USA

Published by Dark Fire Press LLC

The stories, characters and incidents in this publication are entirely fictional. Any similarities to persons (living or dead), events, institutions or places are purely coincidental.

The contents of this book are the © Copyright and ™ Trademark of J. M. DeSantis. All rights reserved.

The Dark Fire Press logo is the © Copyright and ™ Trademark of Dark Fire Press LLC. All rights reserved.

Editor: Susan DeSantis

Cover Illustration: J. M. DeSantis
Cover & Book Layout: J. M. DeSantis

The names appearing on page 59 of this book are of those Patreon supporters of J. M. DeSantis at the time of publication. Their inclusion is a reward for their support.

No part of this publication may be reproduced, stored in a retrieval system, or transmitted in any form or by any means (including electronic, mechanical, photocopying, recording, or otherwise) without prior written permission from the publisher.

Dark Fire Press is a staunch supporter of creators' rights and asks that you respect those rights too. Our authors retain full ownership of their work. Please support the creator(s) by purchasing only authorised versions of this work, rather than support and encourage piracy of copyrighted materials. Thank you.

ISBN (print) 978-1-7346365-4-3
ISBN (digital) 978-1-7346365-5-0

www.darkfirepress.com
www.jmdesantis.com

First Edition: September 2023

# Table of Contents

# Claude

# I

Claude's hand hesitated over the small, silver bell that rested upon the counter of the Green Ivy Inn.

"It dunna bi'e, frien'," said one of the patrons who had taken notice of Claude's sudden pause. "An' neitha' doe' tha goo' innkeepe', tha's a fac'."

Claude's eyes rested upon the man for only a moment, yet to Claude it felt as a great passage of time. He felt the throbbing of his heartbeat in his temples, and the collar of his shirt suddenly felt a size too small. His head began to ache, and he gulped hard. Did the patron notice? How long had Claude been standing like that?

A trickle of sweat began to run down Claude's forehead, and he squinted as it worked its way down to his eye. With that his lip curled, and Claude turned that curl into a smile. My, how good he had become at that.

He let out a slight chuckle to guard against the tremble he felt. The patron smiled back.

"Cheers," said Claude.

"Sláinte!" returned the patron as he raised his glass and gulped down the last of his frothy ale.

The place reeked of it, as though the very air inside the inn were dense with alcoholic humidity. Claude was surprised the candles on the walls and tables did not light the place aflame. Though he supposed the wood would not burn; the wood looked so wet it all appeared to be alive. He could not understand how the small and unremarkable charcoal portrait of a little girl hanging on the wall behind the counter did not fall to mush in its sagging frame. The palm of Claude's hand made a soft sucking sound as he pulled it away from the counter. He was practically half-rats from the fumes alone. But Claude felt the smell was a great deal more pleasing than the rank stench of foetid fungus and rot.

*Ding.*

The bell sounded quite different than the hollow, resonant bells of Areglos, yet it turned Claude's stomach all the same. An acrid burn flowed up his throat. To his left, out of the corner of his eye, Claude took note of three other men some distance away, two of which were deep in conversation. Notably the third man, though sitting with the other two, was not at all engaged in the talk of his companions. Instead he looked straight at Claude. More still, there was something about the man that Claude felt was out of keeping with the surroundings of this little town and its little inn.

Where the other men had great beards, unkempt hair, and simple clothes of woolen stock, the third man, though he wore similar clothing, did not quite fit with these backwoods folk. His clothes hugged his thin frame better than those of the others, in that they were tailored closer to his frame. His hair, also unkempt, did not look so much naturally dirty as much as it was styled to look so. He had no beard, only some stubble not more than a few weeks old, and his eyes were keen. Intelligent. They stood out in a room full of sheep with dull, glintless gazes. The man seemed intently interested in Claude, like a wolf stalking its prey. Claude felt again the slight trickle of sweat upon his forehead.

Almost compulsively, Claude reached for the bell again, though he knew its sound would sicken him once more, when out of the door behind the counter came another potbellied, formidable man with thick muttonchops, no doubt to make up for what little hair grew above.

"Nah nee' te ring i' again, ser," the great innkeeper said. "I's righ' 'ere. Ya' shoul' ken we in 'Amming are a much sim'le folk than you's used in te big ci'y."

Claude almost turned green. He noticed the Wolf cock its head ever so slightly. But Claude barely missed a beat and let out a soft chuckle. Nothing else came up his throat, and he counted himself fortunate for that.

"City? What makes you think I'm from a city?"

"Ooh, jes' te look o'ya," said the innkeeper. "Ya don' qui'e 'ave te righ'...semmary...sembry...oo! Dammi', Low'll, wha' was te wor' ya used?"

"Semblance." It came from the Wolf.

"Sem'lance," said the innkeeper with a nod and smile. "Yeah, tha's te un. A fine wor'."

Claude supposed he did look out of place—more even than the Wolf stuck out. Though his beard was beginning to grow out and his clothes were torn and soiled from two weeks on the road, it couldn't quite hide the make of his more refined clothing: a shirt, vest, slacks, and a coat—he'd long done away with his hat and scarf.

Two weeks...had it been so long? Two weeks ago. The day the resonant bells of Areglos rang for the first time over a month—where once their sound had been heard daily. He felt his stomach turn again, but he managed to twist his grimace into a smile. He was getting better at this.

"Well, if you can point me to a tailor, I'm sure I'll fit right in soon enough," said Claude.

"An' a bar'er, no doubt?" said the innkeeper.

Claude raised his hand to his chin and rubbed the thickening hair. He had never worn a beard before, not even a moustache, despite its popularity amongst his friends and acquaintances. It was already getting too itchy to bear.

"No. I think I'll keep the beard. Seems to be the fashion here in Hamming—"

"Hm. Righ'. Fashi'n," repeated the innkeeper over Claude.

"—and if I'm going to properly become a Hammingman, I should do as the Hammingmen do." Here Claude ventured a side-eye at the Wolf. He usually was not so brave, but he could not help but smile. Yet when he met the cold stare of the Wolf, he quickly looked away, a cold sweat stealing up the back of his neck. "It's true. I am new to Hamming, but it seems like a nice place to settle down for a quiet life."

"Aye," said the innkeeper. "So'en ye 'ave an 'ome 'ere in 'amming? Fammy?"

"No," said Claude. "No home. No family. All alone. That's why I'm here. I'll need a room for some days until I can find proper lodgings."

"An' a goo' meal, too, I'll wager," said the innkeeper. He leaned on the counter and pointed at Claude. "Yous loo' 'alf starved, like summa mon'rel wolf ou' te wild."

Claude was not certain he could keep food down just yet, starved though he was.

"Sure," said Claude, digging in his pockets and placing a handful of coin on the counter. His eye twitched, despite himself. It sounded just a little too close to the sound of a bell. "Send something up if you would, mister...?"

"Ah! Mys mistake, lad. I's forge'in innaductions," said the innkeeper. "Bradaigh. Though, if i's a twis' o' te tongue fer ye, Brad'll do."

"Thank you, Brad," said Claude with a smile. Brad smiled back. "Claude's the name."

"Goo' te mee'tcha," said Brad, reaching his hand out to shake Claude's. As he did, Brad pulled himself forward and looked over the counter. Claude nearly lost his balance and had to brace himself against the sticky countertop to keep from smashing against it. Brad's smile faded, and he looked at Claude again. Claude's face froze.

"No bags wi' ye?"

"No," said Claude, trying his best to smile. "I'm.. .I'm starting fresh in Hamming."

"Hm. Fresh," repeated Brad. He squinted his eyes and titled his head to one side. He still hadn't let go of Claude's hand. The bones in Claude's fingers were beginning to ache. "An' where was i' ye says ye was from, a'ain?"

Claude could feel the slick perspiration on his palm, but it did nothing to help him slip his hand away from Brad's grip. He felt his collar tighten again, and his temples began to throb. He almost began to tremble. He coughed and cleared his throat instead.

"Wincester," said Claude. "Wincester Parva."

For a moment Brad held Claude's gaze. He looked back and forth between Claude's right and left eyes. One then the other. Claude could feel the knuckles of his hand grinding together.

Then suddenly, Brad let go of Claude's hand with a wide smile. The innkeeper clapped hard on the counter and let out a chuckle. Claude sighed. He thought he noticed the Wolf smiling in the corner.

"Winces'er Par'a. Ha!" said Brad. He shook his head and looked straight at Claude again. "I 'aves coosins as live in Winces'er Par'a. Wha's yer fammy name 'ere, Claude?"

Claude almost fainted. He could barely breathe. His temples began to throb again. He felt his eyes begin to sting. He wanted to blink, but when he did his eyes fluttered like a fly's wings.

"Se-Semple," said Claude. "Claude Semple."

"Sem'le. Aye," said Brad. "A nice, sim'le name."

Another pause. Brad continued to gaze at Claude with slightly squinted eyes, the smile on his face so incongruous that his expression gave the impression almost of a growling beast. Claude shifted in place. He felt a cold perspiration on his top lip. He thanked his luck for the fledgling beard that hid it. The Wolf was staring at him again. No smile.

"Pay me no min', Mr. Sem'le," said Brad at length, and he smiled bright and wide once more. "We jes' 'eard tale o' deser'ers on te road."

"W-what do you mean? Deserters? I hadn't heard of any war out this way."

"Ah! I ken tha's te wron' wor'. I ken i' is," said Brad scratching his head. "Bu' folk as cumma ou' o'Kir'lyn tryin' te 'scape."

"Kirklyn?" Claude barely got the word out. His throat felt dry. His voice cracked. He could no longer smell the stale perfume of ale. A fungoid rot seemed to permeate everything.

"Aye," said Brad shaking his head. "Nas'y bu'iness goin' on 'way ou' t'ere. Shurrey ye 'eard?"

*Ava. Cristian.*

Claude tried to hold back his tears.

"Yes," said Claude. His shoulders sank. The Wolf did not seem to miss the fact and leaned forward in his seat. He formed a steeple-like triangle with his hands in front of his mouth, leaning his elbows on the table. His eyes did not blink as they fixed on Claude. "Nasty business, indeed."

Claude hung his head, staring down at the counter, though his mind was elsewhere. He silently thanked the innkeeper for quickly pulling him out of his momentary haze.

"Well, no nee' te dwell," said Brad as he came around the counter. "We all a lon' way from Kir'lyn, thankee. Les' see yer room, Mr. Sem'le, and ge' ye an 'ot meal. A warm bath too, I shoul'a t'ink. Ye' smell o'rotten, Mr. Sem'le, tha' ye do."

Claude was barely aware of what the innkeeper was saying. His mind was on Ava, and he could feel the cool stare of the Wolf following him as the innkeeper lead him out.


# II


The bath felt invigorating, and the food, though Claude had some trouble getting it down, was much needed. He had been so long on the road, so long in a state of barely conscious motion, that he hadn't realised how tired and famished he was until he had arrived at the inn. Still, every time the sound of the bell came up from downstairs, Claude felt the food was all going to come back up. Eventually he abandoned the massive portion to chill on the lone, circular table near the window, having made barely a notable go at it.

A cool breeze came in from the cracked-open window, and it felt soothing on Claude's aching body, warmed from the bath, as he lay on the bed. The weather had been similar on the day he'd left for Hamming. It had rained the day before. Not a horrible storm, but just enough to keep one indoors under circumstances not so dire as Claude's had been. Oh, how he had hated that day. The putrid stench of fungus, and the weeping. Oh! The weeping. And the sinking feeling in the pit of his stomach knowing full well what he was to do the next day: the day the resonant bells of Areglos rang for the first time in over a month. The day the bells rang twice.

Again, the sound of the bell on the inn's counter echoed up from the common room below, barely yet insidiously audible beyond the closed door. Claude's stomach turned and so did his body as he shifted and curled up slightly upon the stiff bed. More comfortable than grass and rocks, but much less so than what he had been used to for most of his life. He wondered if he couldn't procure a softer bed for himself, even amongst these less sophisticated folk. A bed without the black stain of rot. Blankets without a foetid fungoid stench.

He wanted a drink, but he was too tired to move. He didn't want to get up. He couldn't face a room of merrymaking and loud noise. He just wanted to disappear into the black nothingness of sleep. Was that what it was like for them? He hoped it was. No real conscious knowledge of the experience. Just a loss of awareness before the loss of humanity. But those tears running down Ava's cheeks were a harsh reminder of the futility of that hope.

Darkness took him. The bells rang again.

*Ava. Cristian.*

His eyes opened, but all Claude saw was the open window of his room, and the cold, stiff food on the plate on the wooden table beside it. Screams and cries floated up from the streets below, but most of those were filled with joy, some with anger. None were the horrors of those former nights, cold and wet and sweeting with rot.

Claude sighed. He was safe now and far away from the nightmares he had left behind, and he was tired; so very tired.

Claude turned over in the bed, and his eyes grew heavy again, though they stung with tears. The bell rang again downstairs, calling Brad to some new task, and Claude fell asleep with the thought of Ava's rotting face, tears streaming down it, as she pleaded with him not to leave.

# III

Claude slept late but got his start early. A bit of breakfast washed down with a thick stout and followed by another and another. Soon the haunting images of Ava and Cristian faded into a fog, and the room became a blur of laughing faces, stern and concerned, and even the smell of rot was soon drowned out by the stench of piss and ale. Like a punch-drunk fighter, the moment he had ceased purging his stomach upon the floor, he was up for more, stumbling to his place amongst the chaos of the action.

Food was offered over and over again and it was delicious though nondescript, as were those who surrounded him. Names all a confused mess, but the smiles were in aplenty, except for Bradaigh whom Claude could never quite be certain if he had frightened, offended, or upset as Brad often looked upon Claude with downward twisting lips—except of course when Claude sung the old barkeep's praises, as though he were the finest host and cook in all the world. Then Brad would visibly blush, and the drinks came unceasingly, whatever Brad's thoughts on the matter.

At some point or another, unconsciousness took him, deep and sound, with no horrors to visit him. And he woke with a pain in his shoulder as though he had tried to force it through a wall. His neck too stung, though he was certain it was from the aggressive affection his company had elicited from the room below. Food and drink again, and it was all gone in a haze of ribaldry and song. There was no time for nightmares. Even the bell seemed a dull threat in the sea of raucous yells.

The sun rose and fell as did Claude and all the common room with them. His head spun and ached and its only cure was more of the dry, stinging drink and games and songs and dancing mad. And dance Claude did, upon the inn's floor as though it were the deck of a ship at sea, dipping and swaying as it threw him about. And when at last Claude had grown sick to death of sailing, when the punches came in too great a fury, he was down and out to drown in a swollen haze.

# IV

"Ah! Mas'er Sem'le!" said Brad the innkeeper as Claude entered the common room. "Yer lookin' qui'e brigh' th'smornin'. Mus'a been an 'ard roa' frem Winces'er Par'a."

"Indeed," said Claude, but he couldn't help but smile. His head throbbed and his eyes ached. He thanked his luck that even in the sunlit hours the inn was none too bright. He stumbled on uncertain feet, though despite these feelings, he felt refreshed somehow. Lighter.

Only one other patron was sitting at a table in the inn, and he seemed mildly content with his bowl of oats. Though it couldn't have been earlier than noon, a fried scent still lingered in the air, masking even the soiled stench of stale ale that permeated his palate and his clothes. Not that it mattered much considering his plans for the day.

"Bacon?"

"Please," said Claude. "A double serving." Brad raised his eyebrows. "I'm quite starved," added Claude. Already the day was looking up.

"Ayes sure ye are, Mr. Sem'le," said Brad. He placed a heaping plate of bacon in front of Claude who tucked right into it. He didn't touch the dark stout the innkeeper served with it. "Ye were makin'a fair 'tempt a' b'commin' an 'ammingman t'ese pas' few days. Though I dinnae t'ink ye made a goo' many frien's inne end."

Claude paused in the middle of a great mouthful of bacon. It hurt gulping it down, and he wiped a fair amount of grease from his lips, that which didn't further stain his shirt.

"Oh dear. Did I say anything untoward?"

"Not as ha'n't been 'eard roun' 'ere afore," said Brad. "I'm sure i'll be wa'er 'neath te bridge once ye've 'stablished yesself in town. 'ammingfolk are used te fro'eners commin' inna town an' makin' fools o'emsel's. 'amming's comm'na up in te worl'. Summat o' a des'nation. More o' ye ou'si'ers comm'na all a time. So wees small folk is use te i'. Who ken? May'e'll be te nex'

Kir'lyn."

Claude almost choked for the second time on his bacon.

"Beggin' yer par'on, ser," said Brad with a frown. "Aye dinnae mean as Kir'lyn is now. Ne. Tha' woul'no do. As i' were, if ye ta'e me meanin'."

Claude decided to take a swig of the stout after all. Twice, in fact.

"Will'ee be nee'in anyt'ing else?" said the innkeeper.

"Just a recommendation for that tailor," said Claude, "and if you know anywhere that might be letting rooms on a permanent basis?"

# V

Claude wasn't about to let a bit of discomfort that morning ruin his day. He had spent four days mourning his old life. Today was the first day of his new one. And once he had secured permanent lodgings, Claude would make sure to steer clear of the Green Ivy Inn—at least for a while.

Best to look the part, so he decided to start with the tailor. There he was able to procure a set of loose-fitting clothes and put a deposit down for the two outfits that he was measured for. He offered his old clothes up to the tailor for the fabric or to burn them, but the man wouldn't take them for either.

Next it was up to the north end of Hamming where Bradaigh said there were new "'par'men's," coming up in the area. All the newcomers to Hamming were moving into that side of town, and it was, as Brad put it, "a more afined area"—just the sort of place where Claude might find himself a little more at home. Of course, Hamming was still Hamming. Though it was growing with new peoples moving in at an increasing rate, it was only in the beginning stages of this new development. By all accounts, Hamming was still a small town with few of the comforts and refinements enjoyed in city life.

The roads on the East End were still dirt and mud, while to the West some bricks and stones had been laid down to create some semblance of a paved road. What passed for a carriage in Hamming was little more than a farmer's wagon with a makeshift canopy strung up atop it. Still there was potential here, and even if Claude saw little growth in his lifetime, the change of lifestyle was not going to be quite so drastic as he originally envisioned it. There was a boutique, a proper restaurant, an apothecary, and what Claude took to be a hat shop. Though this last establishment did not seem to be faring well, and the windows were darkened. Only one couple in the street appeared to be customers of the shop, and Claude had to admit that their respective top hat and feathered hat looked out of place in Hamming, but given time, the fashion might catch on. All in all, it seemed that Hamming was a strange, eclectic mix of two different eras and cultures, and that suited Claude just fine.

Opposite the aforementioned shops were two thin, three-story buildings. A third seemed to be in the beginning stages of construction right beside the all but abandoned hat shop across the street. The two completed, thin buildings weren't quite the luxurious sort to which Claude was used, but their brown brick facades and multicoloured roofs had a quaint charm to them.

The one on the left had a sign on it stating, in very crude lettering, that no rooms were available. Claude supposed the proprietor of the establishment likely had grown tired of relating the fact to newcomers. Claude shrugged and went into the one on the right. At least the choice was made for him. He supposed it was fate.

He came into a large open room with wooden chairs on either side. Seated in one was an older gentleman, reading a paper and smoking a pipe. It smelled wonderful to Claude. He decided that on his way out, he would ask the man where one might procure a pipe for himself. Sitting down to smoke a new pipe would be just the way to celebrate after finding himself new living quarters.

Just to the left of the staircase, at the back of the large room, was a wooden counter with a ledger, poorly bound and falling apart, and a small, dull metallic bell. Another bell. Claude's jaw tightened as did his chest, so that the air stuck there and it began to hurt not to breathe. Fortunately, there was a sound of footsteps on the stairs, and a voice from above, saving him from this momentary paralysis.

"'Allo!" said a slim man with a pointed goatee and short, receding hair. Thinning yes, but it was all a deep brow with not a hint of white. "I dinna hear the bell." Claude sighed silently with relief that the man's accent was a good deal less thick than Bradaigh's. At least he wouldn't have to learn a new language to make it in Hamming.

"I never rung it," answered Claude. "I had just

walked in."

"Good ta' know," said the man, finishing his descent with a sigh. "Lookin' fer an apartment, then?"

"Indeed," said Claude, and he almost laughed he smiled so hard, so excited was he feeling again. This all seemed so easy for him after all. First the town's changing nature in favour of the lifestyle to which he was used, and now a man offering him just the thing for which he was in the market. His luck was really changing for the better after all the misery of the past few months.

"Yup, well I was 'fraid o' that," said the proprietor, scratching his pointed beard. "I's full up. Last o' 'em went today, jes' an hour agone."

So much for luck.

Claude couldn't believe his ears. Indeed, he refused to. He began to tremble slightly, but he turned that nervous energy into a laugh.

"Oh! Good man! You must be joking."

"I ain't make no jest, ser," said the proprietor squinting his eyes, and he did not return Claude's smile. "An' I don' appreciate you sayin' so. Wee's full up and tha's o' fact."

The man leaned onto one leg and crossed his arms, likely wondering what new accusation Claude was going to make, but Claude was too dumbfounded to notice the man's change in countenance. His luck couldn't have run out this quickly. It was all working out so perfectly. He had gotten this far already. A setback seemed impossible.

"I-I-w-well! Certainly...there must be something available?"

"Didtcha check next door?"

"They've a sign up."

"Well," said the proprietor, and he took a long pause as he looked up and scratched his pointed goatee once more. Claude braced himself against the counter. He felt as though he couldn't stand. Sweat began to bead his forehead. The proprietor took no notice.

"I do hav'a couple is movin' out onnaccount of she bein' wit' child. They're gonna need more room than I canna provide."

"When do they move out?"

"A month. Maybe two?"

Claude's hand almost slipped off the counter. He caught himself, and his hand landed on the bell. It made a dull dinging sound, just enough to turn Claude's stomach.

"A month or two?!" he barely sighed.

"Now don' you go startin' with the salt again, ser," said the goateed proprietor, and he pointed at Claude as he did, "else you can wait for Conner nex' door ta have a vacancy or the new buildin' across the way ta finish. A month or two. I'm sorry, but tha's all I can give ya. Well, unless ol'Samuel over there drops dead this week."

The old man with the pipe barely looked up from his paper. "Beardsplitter."

"He's such a lovely old man," said the proprietor smiling as he looked in old Samuel's direction. Claude just kept looking down and wiped his forehead with his free hand. This time the proprietor took notice, his forehead wrinkling with concern.

"Now, ser," and the smile faded from his pointed face, "there's no reason as ta get so upset about it. You jes' arrive in town, or you stayin' somewhere close?"

"The Green Ivy Inn."

"Ol'Bradaigh's place? Been a while since I've been over thereabouts. Need to go say 'allo."

"I'm thinking about switching to a new establishment," said Claude.

"Well there'as the purpose of yous comin' here," said the proprietor. "But why put yerself through so much movin' about? Seems yous havin' a hard enough time as it is." Claude was still braced against the counter, and his head was bowed again, sweat running down the sides of his face. "I know the lodgings aren't ideal long term, but Bradaigh's a good host. I'll have him strike you a deal on the room, and since I knows jes' were you are, soon as the apartment opens up, I'll call on you at Bradaigh's, a'ight...Mister...?"

"Claude," said Claude. "Claude Rev...eh, Semple. Claude Semple."

"Good, Mr. Semple."

The proprietor held out his hand, though Claude failed to take it. He was staring wide-eyed at the ground. The proprietor paused there a moment and then took the offered hand and clapped Claude on the shoulder with it.

"Easy, Mr. Semple. You've an apartment soon as it's ready. By all accounts, yer an official Hammingman!"

# VI

The prospect of returning defeated to the Green Ivy Inn was a none too welcome one for Claude. And to have to stay for a month or more? He barely knew if he could survive it. Brad's incessant questions were too much to bear. And that Wolf. Who knew when the suspicious man would show up again? Indeed, Claude barely knew if he would survive the day. His head was spotted with sweat, and he felt out of sorts. Dizzy. He swayed a moment to one side, almost losing his balance entirely, as he walked down the main dirt avenue from the West End back to the Green Ivy Inn.

"Semple."

Claude tried to calm himself. It was only a minor setback. No need to get all worked up about it. After all, he did have an apartment; it was merely being held for him was all. Things really were not going all that badly. Then why was it he felt so ill?

"Semple!"

*Was that a bell?* Claude could swear he heard a bell. *Where? One of the stores maybe? Or a man walking his cow to be slaughtered?* Claude's stomach turned. He felt he would wretch. The smell of fungus. Rot. He stumbled. *Ava.*

"Claude!"

At that sound of his name, Claude's mind cleared again, and he righted himself, just in time before stumbling into a poor woman and her little girl. Sweat beaded his skin, but he felt in control of his faculties once more, albeit a bit shaky. The sun seemed bright up above, and he could smell the earth beneath his feet, and something else as well: a faint but growing flowery smell. With slightly aching eyes, Claude turned in the direction of the voice, and there he saw the thin figure in close fitting clothes, the purposely unkempt grey-brown hair, the clean shaven face, the keen eyes. The Wolf.

"'Allo! I saw you at the Inn the other day. Bradaigh's place," said the Wolf as he walked up to Claude. There was a strange odour about the man that Claude could not quite place. Some sort of incense?

"Indeed," responded Claude with little movement about his face but for the parting of his lips to speak.

"Your name? Claude Semple? I have that right?" persisted the Wolf.

They were quite close to one another now, and Claude, having only seen the Wolf from a distance at the Inn, noted that the man wore a peculiar necklace. It looked almost like a fragment of old wood, with a strange rune gilt onto it in some golden-copper substance. The rune had the odd, abstract appearance of a man hanging upside down. Claude felt calm looking at it, and suddenly it seemed the sweat and shakiness were far away.

"I didn't catch yours," said Claude looking up and meeting the Wolf's gaze. He was not usually so bold, but he felt particularly confident with the sudden passing of the worst of his ill-feelings, and he was quite irritated to be standing with the Wolf. He couldn't be certain why he felt suddenly so well and like himself again. It was such a curious necklace the man wore. And that scent. He knew it. It was something Ava used to burn in their home at times.

"Lowell's the name," spoke the Wolf, and he extended a hand outward. Claude did not take it, though he was aware of it.

*Lavender! That was the scent.*

"Pleasure," said Claude through a tightened jaw and gently gritted teeth. The Wolf named Lowell cocked his head and squinted an eye for just a moment. Then he lowered his hand and paused, taking a deep breath and then letting out a soft sigh. His brow furrowed.

"You said you're from Wincester Parva, yeah?" said Lowell. Claude did not respond, but he looked shiftily down at the necklace again. Lowell was so close now, the scent of lavender was sickening yet strangely calming. Claude's nerves and thoughts were all confused. "I thought that's what I heard you tell ol'Bradaigh. It's strange though, isn't it? Your accent, I mean." And here Lowell crossed his arms and let out another soft sigh. "I mean, Wincester Parva isn't quite Hamming, but it would stand out there too. Was there anywhere else you lived for most of your life? Somewhere south? Say—"

But before Lowell could finish the words, Claude lunged forward. He meant to grab Lowell's arm, but something held him back from making such an aggressive move. Something physical, yet unseen, as if an invisible shield surrounded the Wolf. The crowd, Claude thought. That had to be it. He did not wish to cause a scene in front of so many people.

"Listen, man!" said Claude, his eyes blazing. His head throbbed. Why was he so angry? He could not understand, and he seemed constantly on the brink just now of losing control. Perhaps he had overindulged for the past few days. He could almost smell a hint of rotting fungus in the air, but the lavender incense the Wolf wore was doing much to cover it. Claude's stomach turned, but he was so incensed he could not stop himself from continuing.

"I may not know you, but I know where you're from! Your 'accent' doesn't exactly pass for Northern either. And the cut of your clothes is a dead ringer! We both know why you're here, so if you know what's good for you, you'll leave me be! Bring me any trouble or expose me, and I swear you'll not escape either. Mark me!"

And with that, eyes wide and blazing, Claude turned on his heel and continued down the road. It felt wonderful. Claude could never recall in all his life being so brave and assertive. New life, new man. He smiled to himself, though the cold sweat soon returned to his forehead and the trembling in his body slowly grew as he walked. He thought he heard the Wolf howl after him. Something to the effect of: "Claude! You need help, man!"

# VII

By the time he reached the Green Ivy Inn, Claude was feeling nearly as ill as he had been at the apartment building earlier that morning. He kept telling himself to calm down. The apartment would be ready in no time. He managed to maintain control over himself long enough to inform Bradaigh about the situation and that the pointy-goateed gentleman would be by to say hello soon. Brad was "migh'y pleas'te 'ear tha'." Then Brad seemed to have made a comment about how pale Claude looked and said something about a doctor. Claude couldn't keep it all straight.

It was already hard enough following Brad's speech, but it seemed near impossible, feeling so ill as Claude did just then. Claude later recalled that he told Brad he was tired and that he'd had a considerably stressful morning. Perhaps it was all too much exertion after four days of drinking himself blind. Better, he thought, that he had slept in the entire day—but he knew that would have only led to more drinking in the end, even if he did not confess as much to Brad. Claude still wasn't certain he could abide sitting alone with his thoughts. It would do him no good to dwell on the past if he wanted a fresh start, anyway.

Even though it was not quite evening, he was going to return to his room. He asked that he not be disturbed, but that he would be back down when he had rested sufficiently. He did not recall much that followed. Not the stumbling, sore ascent up the stairs, or anything Brad might have said afterward. But he did feel the bed beneath him as he curled up on it, fully clothed, the afternoon sun beating down through the window.

His eyes ached tremendously, and he could barely keep them open. His head swam. He didn't even hear the bell when it finally rang but ten minutes later.

# VIII

Ava, alive and healthy. And there, little Cristian running toward his father, anxious to be placed on his lap. Claude picked him up. It felt strange, that sort of affection, but he went along with it. Only then did he notice the old man standing in the corner watching them. Claude couldn't place the man's face, but he did recognise the smell: the sweet smell of foetid fungus and rot. Then he felt the weight of little Cristian's body shifting. Something unnatural about the feeling of the boy in his arms. Claude looked down. The boy melted into a thick, black sludge, losing all appearance of humanity. The faceless boy dripped upon the floor, blackening Claude's hands as it did.

In horror, Claude stepped back, trying to distance himself from the slime, but it held strong, as though sucking his hands and arms into itself. He looked toward his wife and saw the thick, muscled body, the long mutton chops, and the balding pate. Bradaigh opened his mouth as though to scream, but all that came out were the sound of hollow, resonant bells.

Claude screamed as the slime crawled up his hands and over his arms, but the bells drowned him out, oppressive in their dirge.

"Well, Claude," came a strange voice, breaking the din of the bells, "The fever's bro'e."

Claude squeezed his eyelids tight and then opened them slowly, blinking as his vision adjusted to the light. The sun had barely moved from its place in the sky, yet he could still smell the fragrant scent of fungus.

Claude looked around, barely lifting his head from the pillow beneath. He was still in his room at the Green Ivy Inn, but there were two men there with him. Had they followed him up the stairs? One man was large with a great mustachio and mutton chops. He stood near the door. The other man was standing over him. An older man with chin whiskers and a bald pate. He didn't recognise the second man at all, but the first man...

"But you'll nee'te look af'er yer hand," said the older gentleman.

*Brad! That was the first man's name. Short for...*

"On'y seen one case of et afore," he continued, giving a passing though meaningful glance in Bradaigh's direction. "I lef' some ointmen' fer te spo'. Apply et t'rice a day. I'll call again in a few days. Come by or sen' fer me if et worsens."

He picked up a hat from the foot of Claude's bed and placed it over his glowing, shiny head. *So, the fashion was catching on!* Claude smiled.

The older gentleman walked toward the door and nodded to Brad before walking out. Claude continued smiling as he rolled over in his bed. There was a strange watery feeling in his head. He squinted his eyes as the fluid shifted, like a lake being upset by the pounding tread of a giant.

"My 'pologies, Mr. Sem'le," came Brad's gruff tones from the corner. Claude was aware of a slight throbbing in his head now. "Yer ne'er came doon, and by te nex' night, I grew afeared. Called te doc'or 'gainst yer wishes, bu'ere was not'ing fer et."

Claude groaned. He didn't quite understand what the innkeeper was saying, and the attempt to work out the meaning was making his head throb all the more. With a bit of effort, Claude began to prop himself up in the bed. The fluid in his head shifted again. The pungent smell of fungus stole up into his nostrils.

*Bells? A wolf.*

"Ah! Now dunna exert yerself, Mr. Sem'le," said Brad. "Te doc'or wan's ye te ge' rest."

*Brad was such a funny man. What doctor?*

Claude swung his legs over the edge of the bed and placed his feet on the floor. His back was to Brad. The fluid in his head shifted again. Claude grunted. It hurt, his head, the liquid moving around in it. He shut his eyes tightly once more against the pressure, and he placed his left hand on his face, as though it would help ease the throbbing.

Brad's voice came again from behind, but Claude couldn't make much sense of it. The voice sounded hollow and far away, like there was a great store of water in his ears. He squeezed near the top of his nose, between his eyes, putting pressure on his sinuses to get a reprieve from the pressure in his head. As he pulled his hand away from his face, he finally noticed it: a black, moldy looking spot on the back of his hand, beneath the middle and pointer finger and near to the thumb. From it came a foetid stench.

Claude froze. His eyes widened, and he began to feel a cold perspiration on his forehead once more. He clapped his right hand down over his left, and turned toward Bradaigh. Claude's eyes remained comically wide, but otherwise he made an attempt to appear normal.

"How long was I out?"

"Oh er," said Brad, sighing, "'bout t'ree days. Yous were runnin' qui'te fe'er, Mr. Sem'le. All unconnous an' all."

"Three days!" exclaimed Claude, and he went to stand. Too quickly it seemed. The fluid in his head shifted again, and it seemed to crash about so loudly that, to Claude, it sounded like the waves of the sea were dashing against his skull. A cold, salty sweat began to bead his entire body. He braced himself against the bed, pausing for a moment as the fluid in his brain slowed and steadied. Then he scrambled to find whatever clothes he could and hurriedly made for the door as he spoke.

"An apartment," Claude said aloud as he pulled on a pair of trousers. "I need to find an apartment."

Claude noted the black spot on his hand again, and so immediately tore the sleeve from his old shirt, the one he wore to Hamming, and wrapped the hand so as to conceal the spot. Then he moved to grab a new shirt and jacket.

"Oh. 'Er," was all that came from Brad's stiff and wide-eyed form as Claude finished pulling on his shoes. Claude rose from the bed once more and started for the door. Brad could see the clamminess of Claude's skin, and he began to break out into a sweat himself.

"Oh, M-Mr. Sem'le," stuttered Brad. "Why no'stay a bi'? I 'ear Low'll was on 'is way an' wan'ed te see ye. Check in on how yer doin' an' all."

"No time, man," said Claude as he swayed to one side, catching his balance by bracing against a wall of the room. The sound of the sea. The smell of fungus. It was like walking on a boat in the middle of a storm. "I-I must find an apartment. I've already lost three days. Where can I find one, good man?"

"Well, uh, te Wes' En', Mr. Sem'le," began Brad, and Claude perceived the man looked as if he had been struck, but Claude wasted no time on ruminations. In a flash, he was out the door and down the stairs, Brad's voice going unheard behind him.

"Bu' 'aven' ye...?"

# IX

The walk to the West End was a bit of a struggle at first. Claude kept hearing the incessant crash of waves upon his skull, and his head was beginning to ache from it, making the sunlight difficult to bear. Thrice he stumbled, once into a large man who was kind enough not to get angry, but helped him straighten. Strangely, the man seemed quite concerned for Claude's well-being. Claude merely waved the man off. He was in far too much of a hurry for idle prattle. Too much of a hurry, in fact, to bother stopping in at the tailor he noticed along the way to get fitted for some new Hamming-ish clothing.

When he reached the West End, Claude found it to be a quaint, yet infinitely more refined area of the growing town of Hamming. Here was an effort to bring more of a city atmosphere to the newcomers to town, and Claude found the sight quite comforting. The roads were in the beginning stages of being laid with bricks and stones, not like the dirt roads of the rest of the village. There was a boutique, a proper restaurant, and an apothecary. Claude also noted a building that looked like a hat shop, though its windows were darkened from both a lack of light and a thin film of dust upon the glass. Claude frowned. He would very much have liked to purchase a new hat. He had left his at home.

Next to the hat shop was a building in the beginning stages of construction, and opposite that and the shops were two, thin, three-story buildings. Claude recognised their make well enough and decided to begin with the one on the right.

Just beyond the ascending front steps, the porch, and the front door was a large room with chairs set on either side. One chair in particular was occupied by an older gentleman who was seated reading a paper and smoking a pipe. Claude loved the smell of pipeweed, and like his hat, he missed his own. He decided to ask the gentleman where in town he might procure one—but in a moment. He had more pressing business to attend to first. As if reading his mind, a voice came from behind the counter of the large entry hall.

"Oh! 'Allo," said a slim man with brown, receding hair, and a pointed goatee. There was not a hint of white in it either.

"Greetings, good man," said Claude as he strode up to the counter, returning the goateed proprietor's smile. "I was wondering if there were any apartments available?"

The proprietor looked dead at Claude with parted lips and a furrowed brow. Claude heard the newspaper crinkle behind him and something like a singular, forceful cough. A moment passed in silence. Then the proprietor began to laugh.

"Oh, Mr. Semple," said the proprietor, shaking his head, the broad smile returning to his face. "That trick ain' gonna work. I tol'ye I'd call in abou' a month at te Green Ivy. Maybe sooner."

Claude's brow furrowed. He could feel a cold sweat on his skin.

"I don't know what you mean, man," returned Claude. His head ached, and he grit his teeth. "Is this the Hammingman's way of a jest? I'd like a room, if you have one, else I can take my business next door."

The proprietor squinted his eyes and crossed his arms, leaning back slightly from the counter. There was a shuffle of paper behind Claude. Someone clicked their tongue against the roof of their mouth.

"Now, Mr. Semple," said the proprietor. "I already done tol' ya, I ain' one fer jokin' such way, an' less I apprecia'e ye suggestin' so. Now, if this is ye idea of a joke, ye gon' too far. I ain' havin' it. So leave off 'ere. I ain' wanna star' with a new tenan' on bad terms."

"Then," said Claude, and he placed his left hand on the counter and leaned forward. From beneath the makeshift bandages came a fungoid stench. "I'd appreciate it if you'd let me see what rooms you have available."

"Zounderkite!" came the voice of the older gentleman seated at a distance behind Claude.

"Quiet, Samuel," said the proprietor. "Summat ain' right 'ere."

The proprietor leaned forward now and uncrossed

his arms, though his eyes remained slightly squinted. He looked straight at Claude for a minute or two, studying his face. Claude felt again the trickle of sweat on his brow. He felt dizzy and tired all of a sudden.

"Are ye alrigh', Mr. Semple?" asked the proprietor at length.

"Well," said Claude, an imperceptible tremble beginning to work its way up his left arm. "I do feel a bit..." But Claude didn't finish. He wiped his forehead with his left hand.

"Do ye remem'er anythin', Mr. Semple?" the proprietor continued, his brow furrowing again. "Ye was in 'ere jes three days ago askin' 'bout apartments. I tol' ye it'd be a month or two, maybe sooner, but I'd call on ye at Bradaigh's soon as there was news te give."

"I-I," said Claude, still rubbing sweat from his forehead. The cold, hollow sound of the sea was almost deafening.

"Ye don' look well, Mr. Semple," said the goateed proprietor, "if ye don' mind me sayin' so. Why don' ye go back te yer room at te inn an' 'ave ol' Bradaigh call on te doctor fer ye? Get some res'."

"Y-yes," said Claude. "Yes. Rest. Maybe I will...do just that."

He turned and slowly walked out of the apartment building, rubbing his head all the while. The sound of the sea was so loud now, he didn't hear the proprietor call after him:

"An' 'ave ye a bath. Ye smell o'righ' rotten, ye do."

# X

The sound of the sea was still rushing through his head when Claude smelled a faint hint of incense.

"Claude!" called a voice from behind, and Claude suddenly felt the gentle clap of a hand on his shoulder.

"Lay off me!" came Claude's voice, and he spun around as he slapped the man's hand away with a crack. Then he paused when he looked up and was met with the penetrating gaze of the Wolf. Many of those in the crowded street paused, looking on half-frightened and half-curious at the sudden violent turn that simple day took in their quiet town. The Wolf looked Claude up and down, raising his eyes brows as he did.

"Claude," said the Wolf. "You don't look so well."

"I'm fine, Wolf," but Claude's mind was blank again but for the crash of waves.

"Lowell," said the Wolf flatly. He watched as Claude wiped his forehead. "You know, Claude, I was just on my way to call on you. Brad sent for me. Said you were in a bad way. I was concerned."

"What do you care?" said Claude with a grunt. His head pounded. He squeezed his eyes shut and pinched their corners with his fingers. The waves were deafening.

"Listen," said Lowell, leaning in and lowering his voice. The crowd was already moving on by then, giving up the possibility of some rare excitement, but Lowell didn't seem to want to call any additional attention to the situation. "Claude. I have to go away for a bit. Urgent matter. Why don't you come with me? Whatever's going on with you, I promise, we can help."

Claude looked up. His eyes were wide. Lowell continued, inching toward Claude bit by bit.

"Hi, there! What happened to your hand?"

Lowell reached out to touch Claude's roughly bandaged hand, but he barely got near to it when Claude's eyes suddenly blazed with manic hatred. For the second time he slapped Lowell's hand away.

"No!" Claude screeched and then punched Lowell square in the jaw, though he pulled it just at the end of his swing. A strange sensation ran through his body as his fist neared Lowell, but the suddenness of the attack was still effective in knocking the unsuspecting and otherwise formidable Wolf back a few steps. Blood tickled from Lowell's split lip, but Claude took no notice, nor did he of the crowd which had gathered to see the cause of the commotion. He suddenly felt a great desire to be away from the strange glow emanating from Lowell's chest. A few people from the crowd rushed to Lowell's side and were helping him to his feet. Claude pushed through the few onlookers that otherwise barred his way, and he ran all the way back to the Green Ivy Inn, swaying and stumbling as he went.

# XI

The door of the Green Ivy Inn slammed hard against the wall, and Bradaigh looked down at the crumpled and staggering form of Claude. With a groan and a sideways sway, Claude rose to his feet, holding his head with his hands.

"Mr. Sem'le?" said Brad, at a loss for words otherwise.

Claude came forward, slammed hard into a table, rocked sideways and braced himself against the edge of another. He looked like a man trying to walk a short distance on the deck of a ship caught in the middle of a storm. The waves in his head were so strong now after his mad dash back to the Inn. Claude tried to take a deep breath as the sea quieted.

"Mr. Sem'le?" came Brad's voice again. Claude let out a sigh. His head throbbed, waves or no, and Bradaigh's incessant prattle wasn't helping the matter.

"I need to rest, Brad," Claude finally managed. He stepped forward and swayed on his feet again. "I saw your man, Luger."

"Low'll."

"Right," said Claude. "If he comes here looking for me, you tell him I've switched to another inn." Claude almost stumbled into the counter as he continued forward. "Or left Hamming altogether. But don't let on that I'm still here and don't send him up under any circumstances. Do you understand?" And here Claude, leaned on the counter and looked, as best he could manage, straight at Brad.

"Well, er, y-yes, Mr. Sem'le, bu—"

"Good man," and with that, Claude continued on his way up to his room.

"Shoul' I call te doc'or, Mr. Sem'le?" shouted Brad after him.

But Claude did not answer. *Just after some rest*, he thought to himself. He struggled and stumbled the rest of the way up, scraping his shoulder against the wall of the narrow stair in an effort to stay on his feet. When Claude reached the top, he pushed through the door of his room. He dropped his jacket right there on the floor and made his way to the bed. When his head was down, after an initial spin that almost sent him vomiting upon the clean sheets, the waves ceased to sway for the first time all day. Thankful for the fact, Claude sighed and closed his eyes. He quickly drifted off to sleep.

# XII

When Claude awoke, it was already night. He felt the cool air drifting off the waves outside his window. From downstairs he heard the ring of the dinner bell. There was an uncomfortable feeling in his stomach. It made him sad, though he did not understand why.

His stomach made a noise, and Claude considered that the feeling in his stomach simply meant that he was hungry. Slowly he rose up from the bed. There was a strange sense of floating, not as though through air, but rather like he moved beneath the surface of a great body of water. His movements seemed likewise slow and unsteady. At times a simple motion even felt like it was done with a great effort against an encumbering force, yet without any true sensation of gravity. But the inherent desire to feed himself and the faint, delicious smell of food drove him onward through the invisible force and toward the stairs.

As he moved, Claude was faintly aware that his

vision had changed. For some odd reason, his entire perception of depth and distance seemed inconsistent. Though he didn't much try to make sense of this. He was too hungry. On he went, through the door and down the stairs, following the direction of chattering voices, the mouth-watering aroma of food, and the occasional light ring of the bell.

When he reached the bottom of the steps and came into the common room, Claude saw that two men were laughing at either side of the counter. The man on the inside of the counter was tall and thick, with a quite admirable set of mutton chops. The other man was quite a deal younger, with reddish hair and freckles. Claude smiled to see the two men laughing and enjoying themselves as they did. He decided to inquire of those two amicable gentlemen about some food. But Claude had hardly taken two steps forward when the two men noticed him and turned, and he saw that the healthy colour of their faces faded to a sickly pale, and their eyes went wide. The large gentleman let out a gasp, whilst the younger man gripped the edge of the counter and grit his teeth. Hardly had Claude marked their responses, when a shrill, gut-wrenching cry cut through the air, and what little talk was going about in the room went dead silent.

All eyes were on Claude now and the one who uttered that scream, the woman, sat stiff with tightened lips and wide, watery, and reddening eyes. At that moment, Claude unaccountably reached up to touch his face, and at that touch, he too stiffened with terror. His body began to shake, and he felt the sting of tears in his eyes—rather, his eye. Claude turned and raced back up the stairs to his room, stumbling into the walls as he did, though they were his only source of balance. Behind him he heard Bradaigh's voice say "Oh, dear...," and all the whispers and cries which followed it were blissfully drowned out by the closing of the door to Claude's room.

No, thought Claude, as he leaned against the door, panting heavily and trying to steady the fluid feeling in his head. He looked down at his left hand and saw that the blackish mark had spread to his fingertips and halfway up his arm, adding to them small and yellow-greenish abscesses and carbuncles. The stench of rot and fungus filled his nostrils, and so nauseating was it, and so terrified was Claude that he wretched, spilling acrid bile upon the floorboards, which was tinged with a strange discolouration. But Claude did not have time to waste, and staggering to his feet, he moved immediately to the chair and table by the window.

The window he closed and the chair he wedged beneath the doorknob of the room. The table he placed haphazardly next to the chair. These were light enough to carry. Then he moved to the bed.

At the first push, Claude struggled a bit and his head began to feel the swaying motion of the liquid in it, but he continued to push, occasionally losing his grip or swaying and falling to one knee. Sweat began to bead on his skin once more, and once or twice Claude stopped to let the waves which crashed against his skull silence and calm.

*Damn it*, thought Claude, *where was Cristian?* He could really use the boy's help at the moment.

Eventually, Claude managed to push the bed against the chair and he felt at once nauseated. The waves were crashing hard against his head now, his brain feeling like a ship caught in a storm on a vast open sea. He laid down upon the bed, trying to steady his breathing and calm the raging storm. His last thoughts were of the rotting visage of Ava, and with it came the smell of foetid fungus.

# XIII

Sweet was the salted smell of the sea, and Claude felt as though he were floating in its cool, soothing arms. Though nowhere could Claude see the waters of which he felt a part. A window. Perhaps there.

He floated toward it and looked out to see naught but the sun above a burgeoning town, and farmlands in the distance. Perhaps the sea was further on still. Claude pushed forward, but met up against an unseen barrier. He forcefully tried to move past it, but the guardian held fast.

Suddenly, Claude felt an uncontrollable rage steal over his entire body. He punched the unseen foe and heard its strange scream as it bit his hand in retaliation. Claude reeled backwards and slammed against something hard which only roused his anger more. He trashed and flailed, attempting with any of his appendages to do damage to his assailants. Few hit their mark, and they bit at him as much as he at them. Many more of his bludgeoning attacks met naught put open water. The sound of chaos and waves crashed about him.

After a good deal of damage, more to himself than

the entities which taunted him, he found himself standing in the swaying, cool waves of the sea once more. His limbs grew painfully weary, despite the light, weightlessness of the sea. He could hardly breathe, but it had naught to do with being out of the water. He could still hear and feel it around him, and the rage began to calm as the undulating waves took him. He sighed and darkness closed around him.

# XIV

Black and cool were the deepest parts of the sea. Unless there were some illuminate creatures here, nothing of the surroundings could be seen. But it all could be felt. Sensed. It was as womb there: comforting and safe. No predators, aquatic or otherwise.

He reveled in the undulating motions of his body as he floated backwards and forwards, left to himself and away from all irritants. There was no sound in the deep black but for the occasional, faraway, muffled speech of the fishermen above—curious talk—and a bell ringing to call the ships home. He recalled those sounds as familiar, likely on those trips nearer the surface.

Very occasionally, he would butt up against something, and either move in the opposite direction or in the case of a sensation of pain or even discomfort, strike his attacker, to mixed results. Mostly he merely enjoyed the sensation of the cool sea water around him, alone and unbothered. He felt he never wanted to leave his quiet, safe, deep home.

# XV

"How long has he been in there?" came a muffled voice through the blackness. At its sound, he was aware of a mix of anger and trepidation. Though he did not understand the speech in full, he had the vague inclination it once held meaning.

"Since te day ye lef'," came a second, gruff voice from the dark. This one in particular seemed to annoy him. There was a sighing sound, faint but audible, and then the gruff tones came again. "I figurt 'e'd be safe locked up 'ere until ye'd return'd." Another pause, and then. "If ye 'ad stay'd..."

"I'm sorry, Bradaigh. It couldn't be helped, regrettable though our friend's situation has become."

"An' elsewhere?"

Another pause.

"Don't ask, friend. Better not to know. Best we just concentrate on the task at hand."

"Will'ey be able te 'elp 'im?"

"I don't know. We'll do the best can."

"Jes' like Bridgette..."

"Worse, I'm afraid. You haven't seen it like this. I'm sorry to have to put you through this again, Bradaigh."

"No, i's all right. Be'er me t'an sommun' as unawares. I'm 'appy te be o'service. Dumb luck, I s'pose t'at 'e walk'd in te me inn like t'at. Dumb luck."

"Or fate..."

There was another long pause. No sounds but the lapping of water around him. He allowed himself a moment of calm. The darkness took him again. He felt safe. And then:

"C'mon then. Let's crack on."

He heard a noise like taps against wood. Again the trepidation. Fear rose in him. He wondered if he should not swim away and hide or stand and fight this new threat. With the fear, a rage rose in him, primal and impossible to ignore.

"Er...Mr. Sem'le?" Again, a thrill of annoyance.

"Oh, come on now, Bradaigh. You know that's not his real name, and it'll be a miracle now if he'll answer to anything at all."

Then the same voice came again loudly.

"Claude! It's Lowell! I've got Bradaigh—Brad—here with me!"

A chill ran through him. Not the chill of the water, but something else. Something that stirred from his insides and worked its way up out the back of him.

"We're here to help, Claude! Please open the door, if you would!"

He did not move, but floated silently in the water. There was silence for a moment. Then came the gruff voice again. This time it too was loud.

"C'mon now, Mr. Sem—Claude! I knows ye's scar'd, may'ee even a bi' confust. An' we do's care an' all, bu' well, we's can't as 'ave ye spreadin' yer sickness on te ot'ers in 'amming. Bu' Lo'ell 'ere'll take'ee te some'ere safe. Some'ere ye can 'opefully get 'elp. Like 'e did fer my poor lil'Bridgette."

Silence.

"Claude?"

More silence, and then he heard the sound of wood

and metal being force-ably moved about in a tight space. A dull, monotonous thudding followed by a sigh.

"Damn. He's got himself locked up in there well-tight. There's nothing for it, Bradaigh. Let's have it down. We'll pay for the repairs."

There was a loud banging of wood. Bang. Bang. Bang. Again and again and again. Something heavy was slamming hard against something wooden in the dark, and he felt an uncontrollable rage steal over him as the obnoxious banging continued. His head throbbed with pain at each bang. The darkness began to turn red.

With a cracking and splintering sound, the door burst asunder and with it flew pieces of the old wooden chair that once decorated that room at the Green Ivy Inn. Bradaigh hardly noticed it or the bed which had been torn to shreds in what seemed to him like a blind rage. As the large, mutton-chopped innkeeper stumbled into the room, he looked up to behold the horrible visage of his guest, and seeing it, all of the colour left Bradaigh's face. He nearly lost his footing when the muscles in his legs pulsed electrically and his heart began to race.

At once the thing slashed at the innkeeper with a claw-like, rotting limb, tearing through the flesh of the man's shoulder. Bradaigh cried out in agony and reeled backward as the thing came on, flailing its fungoid claws in blind violence.

With great force, Bradaigh smashed backward into Lowell, and as he did, Bradaigh reached out in a feeble effort to steady himself, but his hand only caught on Lowell's curious, rune-gilt necklace, and the force of

Bradiagh's fall tore it from Lowell's neck.

Lowell's eyes went wide and a cold sweat swiftly stole over his entire body. He grabbed for the necklace, but the thing was already on him. It clawed for his face and throat with impossible accuracy for a creature with no eyes. With a slam that knocked the wind from his lungs, Lowell fell backward to the floor, half out of the doorway, as the thing fell on top of him. Lowell struggled against the force of the thing's attacks, doing his best to catch his breath, as he attempted to grab hold of the thing's wrists—or what otherwise passed for wrists.

Inside the room, Bradaigh rose to his feet with a grunt and a moan. He cracked his back as he straightened. There was a sharp pain along his upper back, and his mind was all in a fog. He tried to shake the haze out, but that only seemed to make things worse, and he nearly lost his balance again for the effort. Then he heard the screams coming from the doorway where his friend was lying beneath the lunatic horror that assailed him.

Despite his lumbering size, Bradaigh moved quickly. He took up a large piece of wood from the broken bed and with three strides of his great legs, Bradaigh was behind Lowell's attacker.

Over the hideous, rotting, bulbous thing in the semblance of a man, Lowell saw Bradaigh raise the wooden post above his head with two hands, a wild look in the man's fear-filled eyes.

"Bradaigh! No!"

But it was too late. With crushing force, the massive

innkeeper brought the wooden post down upon the fleshy, gelatinous sack that passed for a head, and with a soft squish, the thing burst open like a piece of overripe fruit, splashing about the brains, bile, and liquefied-bones of the thing that had once called itself Claude Semple.

# Evelyn

# I

velyn looked up from the pulpy ruin of her foe as Barrett brought down his spiked mace upon the head of the last of a small group of infected they had happened upon. The sack caved and the thick viscera of the once-human thing fell to the ground. A spray of blackish blood splashed against Barrett's face. That was precisely why the Reapers wore masks since the early days. Though Evelyn was unclear whether it had any curative properties, the standard lining of frankincense did much to mask the stench of foetid rot and fungus.

The Lunatic Rot. That was the name given to the plague which first appeared in the city of Kirklyn almost three years ago. A family by the name of Greene, if Evelyn recalled correctly, over in the Western Quarter. At the time no one had the slightest idea of the strange nature of the disease which took the Greene's only son and then the Greenes themselves. It was an isolated incident, but then, three weeks later, three more families showed the same signs. Hallucinations and temporary amnesia, then the dreaded blackened skin and puss-filled growths which ended in the terrible disfigurement of the afflicted and their lunatic, violent rage. Left untreated, the heads of the infected would turn into fleshy sacks and grow to the point of near-bursting, so that even the slightest prick would send their fluids gushing into the air. That proved a certain way for the disease to spread, but also the only way to dispense of the most violent of them who were too far gone to send to the Church for treatment.

Otherwise, none knew of the origins of the horrific plague or by what other means it spread. But that was the purpose of their mission, was it not?

*And Mavis.* Evelyn had to find Mavis.

Barrett was good, Evelyn had to admit, but sloppy. All flash and no strategy, but that was the way of the ill-conceived Brave Reapers—the very attribute which helped to earn them the unceremonious title of "Cabbage" among the two other Reaper lodges.

It was little surprise that the Cabbage Reapers had been all but killed off a year ago, when the Lunatic Rot became epidemic in Kirklyn, and the Church Reapers finally welcomed the assistance of the others without scorn. Barrett was the very last of the Cabbage Reapers now, and despite his formidable size, it was a wonder he had survived for so long. Evelyn supposed luck counted for something.

Barrett staggered backward against the stone wall of one of the buildings along the avenue. Slowly he slid down the half-fungoid, blackened-brick and placed his mace on the ground beside him. He pulled off his mask. It looked like a torture device, metal and with no mouth or nose holes for breathing. Only the eye holes for seeing. It was a horrible choice for general battle or Reaping, but again that was the way of those "Brave" ones. The face beneath it was just as unpleasant, but Evelyn supposed that wasn't a fair remark. Mavis, after all, wasn't what someone would call handsome in a conventional sense.

"Barrett! Put your helmet back on and get your bloody ass up, cunt!" said one of the other Reapers.

This one wore all red, a feathered cap, and a porcelain mask designed to look like a skull. Evelyn always thought Miles a bit flamboyant. All fashion and little protection. But Miles was quite formidable, there was no doubt. In fact, all of the remaining twenty Reapers were skilled, she supposed. They had to be to have survived this long. Else they had the seeming good fortune of "Brave" Barrett.

"Oh! C'moff it, Miles!" groaned Barrett. "I'm 'xhausted and there's still a ways to go a'fore we reach the church."

"Cathedral," drawled Miles, and Evelyn could see that his eyes narrowed beneath the deathly visage. Flamboyant and a lunatic—even without the Rot. "And you might not overheat so much if you dressed lighter. Proper training would have taught you that, but I suppose it's to be expected from a Cabbage."

That got Barrett to his feet. He leaned on his mace as he steadily rose to meet Miles's gaze. His mask was still off. Barrett's mouth smiled; his eyes did not.

"Eh, now there, Miles," said Barrett as he scratched his chin, "that's the problem wit' ye Church Reapers.

You're all high and mighty, actin's though you's got all the answers. But you's all come up as done and wrong as the rest. More so, I'd say. Maybe you should as spend more time trainin' 'stead o' tailorin' finery. More'en half these here fell to my mace."

Evelyn noted a subtle twitch in Miles's eyes. The skull-masked man stared at Barrett for a moment, and Barrett looked back.

"Though, I will say, your killin's a thing to be in awe of," said Barrett, letting out a chuckle. "Somethin' perhaps these two could learn from." And here Barrett tilted his head toward the two remaining members of their party.

The two young and—Evelyn supposed—green men, late to enter the ranks of Reapers. *After Uncle Bram.* Evelyn didn't know much about them. They had been from the third lodge, the Cleansing Reapers, before the three lodges became one.

"Did either of ye two fell even one infected since we set out?" said Barrett now turning full to face the two young men. Boone and Russell. That was their names. They looked back at Barrett with blank stares.

Boone was a bit shorter than Russell. He wore a tricorn hat, a silver mask and a short coat. He carried a crescent-shaped sword with him—an unusual design. Russell was lanky but muscular. He wore a scarf around his face, a coat slightly longer than Boone's, and he carried a long, heavy-looking hammer. His bright red hair was unadorned. This was about the only standout feature between the two young men; otherwise they were perhaps the least remarkable of the remaining Reapers.

Evelyn had noticed as much when they had all gathered nearly a week ago. It was about the only remarkable thing about them: how well they faded into the background and could be forgotten.

Miles's eyes narrowed once more as his attention turned to the two young men. Barrett's jaw tightened ever so imperceptibly. Evelyn decided it was finally time to step in.

She shook the tainted blood from her long, thin sword and put it in its sheath as she stepped toward the four men—the sword was the only weapon she carried aside from the pistol strapped to her boot. The click of the sword into place, subtle but pointed, seized the men's attention better than any words might, but it was the sight of Evelyn which held their attention better than any sword might—it always was.

Even beneath her triangular hat, the long coat she wore, and the cloth pulled up over her face, Evelyn's thin, lithe figure was quite apparent. She had a large set of eyes and what might be termed a perfect bone structure and proportion of features. Radiant was a word many used to describe her. At least that was the only word the men spoke that she found flattering. It might have annoyed her more if she wasn't so confident that she could out fight any of them—except maybe Mavis, but then again, Mavis never gawked at her the way the others did. She imagined the fact that she was so capable only turned them on even more. It was frustrating, but there were more pressing matters to be concerned with than the unwanted attention of a few horny men.

"Leave them be," said Evelyn in her cold, measured

voice. "It will do us no good to have dissension amongst us now, regardless of our original affiliations." Mavis. "We can rest ahead, Barrett, once Areglos is in sight." Evelyn was beginning to wonder if she'd chosen the wrong men to accompany her. She began to walk ahead of the others but was stopped by the voice of Barrett.

"Is it really even worth all this trouble?"

*Yes! Mavis is worth everything.*

"It's been three days since we've seen an uninfected." continued Barrett. "Why not jes abandon Kirklyn to rot?"

"This has already been discussed," said Evelyn, turning toward Barrett with a cool glance. Those heavy lidded eyes the men found so seductive, yet equally so intimidating.

"What would a Cabbage Reaper know about honour and duty?" said Miles with a scoff.

Boone and Russell remained silent.

"I know 'bout sense and strategy," returned Barrett, seemingly at Mile's comment. "How do you think sommun as I stands 'ere, the last of the Brave Reapers? I say we abandon Kirklyn and warn the poor souls outside of the city on our way to peaceable lives far away from this nightmare."

"The plan—" began Miles.

"To hell with the plan," interrupted Barrett. "The others very well may have abandoned their duties. We could jes as well slip off and none would be th'wiser."

Evelyn had to admit, she had considered the possibility. That is once—

"We have to know what is happening," said Evelyn.

*I have to find Mavis.* "How else are we to stop the Rot from spreading beyond Kirklyn if we haven't learned at least that much?"

"And what answers do ye think we'll find, pray? What'll be good enough to end this mad obsession fer knowledge fer good and all. A mere twenty of us remain. Mavis, Oscar, and your uncle all had knowledge, all were veteran Shields of the Church. If this were stoppable, they'd have done it."

He was right, she knew it now as much as then when they all discussed the plan, but if she had let doubt enter her heart then or now, they would all perish for sure. And she couldn't leave Mavis. She had to believe that all of the Reapers were holding to their oaths. She had to believe Mavis was all right. She had to believe this lunatic-nightmare would end. She turned and began to move forward once more.

"We've been operating in the dark for months," said Barrett.

"Hence we've banded together to shine light on this all," countered Evelyn.

"Things are worse than before we banded together. You must believe there's no one left at Areglos either," called Barrett after her. "No answers to find there."

No. She had to believe quite the opposite.

She had to believe Mavis was still alive.

# II

Evelyn and her four companions continued through the rain-slicked streets of Kirklyn. A pale moon illuminated the thinning fog, casting a foetid, charnel light over the dampened stones of the city. It had rained two days before, and the storm had moved West, but the sun never seemed to shine on Kirklyn anymore, and a fog was often seen day and night. Rumour was the wide, depressed land beyond Stowshaw used to be a lake, even an inner sea, but even their histories had no details to support that idea, so long had it been dried. The theory was merely the speculation of bored philosophers and archaeologists looking to make a name for themselves. Otherwise, Kirklyn was so far inland, it was strange to imagine there could be so much moisture in the city—but there it was.

On rare occasions—such as on that very night—the fog of the day thinned and even the sky was relatively cloudless by comparison. Evelyn counted their good fortune, as the light would help them to see better in the oppressive dark. Moreover, she could not help but note the natural beauty even of that forbidding moon, so long had either it or its golden brother been denied the vision of the people of Kirklyn the past two months. Ever since the situation in Kirklyn reached its most dire. Ever since Mavis went to Areglos.

The cold, bright light glittering against the stones gave Evelyn a strange hope. It was almost as if the city itself resisted the corrupting, fungal rot which began even to infect the very architecture of Kirklyn.

Here and there choking, black vines and foetid moss grew about the stone walls and slate roofs of the blue-white city, and even the cobbled streets were in places engulfed in the ineffable corruption. Some buildings even were so infested with the stuff that from the decay of rot they began to crumble and cave. But they had all seen worse in the long-quarantined West Quarter. In that long-abandoned section of the city and in bits of the North, the fungoid corruption reigned unchallenged over its growing kingdom.

The five Reapers avoided the infected landscape wherever they could, uncertain how many of the sack-headed creatures might lie about, hidden from sight. They knew detection by even one might bring on the attention of hordes of others. Despite their combat proficiency, five Reapers against a horde of infected was a scenario that was tested in the past, with a greater number given to the Reapers, and to the latter's great failure. It was amazing the raw, unchecked strength of the lunatic infected had, and the things which would set them into a rage was strangely inconsistent. Else, the infected wandered about aimlessly in their half-human shapes, waiting for the ultimate death of their overripe, exploding head, or to be harvested ere that could happen. But the Harvesting had stopped when Areglos closed itself off for good. That was when the Cabbage Reapers fell and those mysterious, unnameable creatures began to appear.

Evelyn was the only known witness to them—that is the only one who had not been driven mad and had lived to tell the tale. Despite the weird happenings in

Kirklyn, none of the other Reapers quite believed her, at best mocking her in hushed conversations, and at best openly half-jesting she had contracted the Lunatic Rot herself. She supposed being desirable to men and the niece of Cleansing Reaper Bram had its uses—else she might have lost her position as the leader of the remaining few when she spoke of the shambling, worm-like creatures she had seen that night. If only Mavis had been there to hold her.

# III

At length, the spired roofs of the Church of Areglos peeked over the horizon. The small band of Reapers came to a halt. They stood now in the very center of the city. There the old fountain—which had, in origin, been built as a sign of Kirklyn's glory—had been broken down many and replaced with a once-worshiped monument. Evelyn could not quite recall what the old fountain had looked like. She was barely more than nine when construction on its replacement had been completed. Miles likely remembered the place as it stood before. He was old enough. And Mavis. Oh, Mavis for certain would remember.

Evelyn looked up at the seven cold visages of the men dressed in Church-like garb, carrying weapons and crosses. The middle-most man held nothing, but rather had his hands turned upwards in a gesture of peace and healing prayer. Lower down, but still on the stone platform, four people prostrated themselves before the seven church warriors, their faces unseen, but one could easily identify them as a man, a woman, a boy, and a girl.

It had been an inspiring sight to Evelyn in her youth, as it had for many who went on to become Reapers. That is, before the mold began to steal up its awe-inspiring forms. Strange how the moss made the figures look more alive now than when the stone was clean. Alive, yet dying all the same, whereas before the clear white stone gave the figures an untouchable and eternal strength.

Evelyn looked down at the plaque that was attached to its base, still largely unobstructed by the living Rot. Though she knew its words by heart:

**Shields of the Church**
**For the Fallen of Stowshaw and the Veterans Thereof**
**Dedicated to the Countless Lives They Saved**

*In truth, what had they saved us from?* thought Evelyn. Her eyes moved down to the smaller letters carved below:

**Dwayne Farver, stone mason**
**Gabrielle Mack, sculptor**
**Made possible with the gracious patronage of Jeff**
**Stoner, Misha Malcolm, Ian Sniffen, Hakan Tandogan,**
**Amanda Rosa, Robert Williams...**

The last few names were scratched out. Little did it matter. They all had perished, Evelyn knew, taken by the Rot. Even those who built this monument could not tell the tale of the old fountain now. A plague had come to

Kirklyn despite that legendary victory in Stowshaw.

Evelyn's thoughts went to Mavis, his tangle of grey hair, the constant stubble on his chin, the kind yet haunted look in his eyes. She wondered if when she saw him again that darkness would be deeper now when suddenly a scream cut through the night.

# IV

"Silence her screaming! There are infected all about. You'll draw their attention."

The man put his hand over his daughter's mouth, gently, kindly, but firm enough to keep another wail from escaping the child's throat. Her brother stood behind the two. All three were huddled in a corner of a small, modest home. No fire burned on the hearth, and though the place looked clean enough, it was a cold and lonely place. There was very little light on account of the windows being boarded up. The walls and floor were bare of decoration. Little evidence of food was there either but for a small crate from which poked a few loaves of white bread—stale as stone.

"Jes' get on with it. We ain't seen an uninfected in three days. There's no way they don't have the Rot in 'em."

"We're not infected. Please. My wife died of the Rot three months ago, but neither me nor the children have shown any signs."

"Miles, please. Put the pistol away."

It was Boone who spoke last, softly, from behind his

silver mask. He was standing to the side of the father and his two children, yet close enough to be between they and the red-cloaked, skulled visage of Mad Miles. The man in red held out a flintlock pistol and aimed it toward the family. Barrett stood eyeing the family with a furrowed brow. Russell stood back a bit from the scene, but kept a keen watch on Barrett and a tight grip on the handle of his great hammer.

"Miles," came Boone's voice again, "at least check them for spots."

Miles narrowed his eyes, but did not take them from the family huddled before him.

"Miles, stop!"

Evelyn entered through the open door of the home. Her sword was drawn, but when she realised there were no infected in the structure, she returned her sword to its sheath.

"They're infected, Evelyn," said Miles. "We cannot allow them to leave here."

Miles had gone mad. Evelyn knew it. Not with the Rot. The man had always been a tad unstable. But now? Why did she take him with her? He could have gone to the Eastern Quarter to the bastion set up there, or better yet on the road West to—

"We don't know that without checking them first," said Boone. "And if you shoot them, you're going to draw the attention of those who are infected."

Miles paused a moment. He sighed and put his pistol away. Then his hand went to the hilt of his sword. Evelyn saw the cold stare in Boone's eyes through his silver mask, saw the hands of Russell tighten around his hammer from the corner of her eye. She moved forward quickly and placed a hand on Miles's arm—the one holding his sheath. The man wheeled around with a wild look in his eye. As mad as the infected, and yet somehow even less reasonable at times. He had taken his role as a Reaper far too seriously. Devout and fanatical, paranoid, and constantly on edge. The minds of men like Miles were always warped by such circumstances as the climate in Kirklyn.

"I said stop," said Evelyn, meeting Miles's wild gaze. Her stomach turned when she looked into his eyes, but she dared not look away, dared not give even the slightest telegraph of her discomfort. Now she remembered: *to keep an eye on him.* That's why he was here.

She felt Miles struggle against her grip. He was strong, dangerously so, but so was she. Eventually, she felt his muscles relax. Internally, she sighed. Externally, she kept her cool eyes locked on him. She saw the tense forms of the family calm in unison with Miles.

"I'll check the girl," said Evelyn. "Boone, you and Russell, the boy and their father."

"Thank you," came a hoarse whisper from the father.

"No trust for Barrett and I, Evelyn?" said Miles. His skull mask smiled at her with its toothy grin. Her eyes had never left him.

"I trust you to fight well when the need arises," said Evelyn after a carefully timed space.

Miles let out a mad, mirthless laugh.

# V

Outside the small home the men stood waiting for Evelyn and the girl. The boy and his father stood off to one side with Boone and Russell. Barrett sat on the masonry of a nearby building that had crumbled nearly to dust. Miles leaned against the stone outer wall of the family's home.

"You know, Cabbage," said Miles. "I'm beginning to find you the most tolerable of this small outfit of ours."

Barrett looked up at Miles with smoldering eyes and a furrowed brow. His jaw tensed. Just then, Evelyn and the girl walked out the front door and onto the cobblestone street.

"Not a spot," said Evelyn.

"Are you certain you were thorough?" asked Miles with a tinge of sarcasm. Evelyn did not rise to his taunt, though she felt her blood boiling.

"And the men?" continued the female Reaper.

"Clean," said Boone.

Miles scoffed. Evelyn walked the girl over to her father and brother. The man stepped toward Evelyn.

"Thank you, again," said the father.

"There are ten Reapers stationed in the Eastern Quarter," said Evelyn. "Take the children there. They won't know you're coming, but there's a password we give to the uninfected to gain sanctuary there." *So they won't kill you on sight.* A second reason why Miles was chosen to accompany her. "As soon as you enter the Eastern Quarter, there will be eyes on you. Speak aloud—"

But Evelyn's voice was cut off by a second terrible cry in the night—only this time there was in its timbre an unworldly and inhuman sound. Just then, the fog passed thick over the moon, and all of Kirklyn was thrown into near pitch darkness.

The family began to shake. Evelyn could smell a sweet, acrid stench. She felt her whole body tighten, and she almost lost her balance where she stood. The blood was rushing from her head.

The scream came again, less aggressive, and loud, but much nearer than before. Then too could be faintly heard the weird, unearthly piping sound being uttered from an uncounted number of hellish throats. They all heard it, not just Evelyn this time. She could see it in their eyes. The men turned to face her.

"That piping..." said Barrett, rising to his feet, and clutching tightly to the handle of his mace.

"So," said Miles looking blindly out into the darkness around them, "it would seem the rumours are true."

Yes. Evelyn alone had the barest inkling of how desperately they needed to get away. She spun on the father and his two children. She attempted not to show the trembling fear that was rising in her body, so as not to terrify the family to madness. The man's returned gaze did not convince her of her success.

"Run! To the East! Go!"

"But..." said the man, "the..."

Another screech from the unseen horrors of the dark.

"Evelyn!"

Evelyn shoved the man. Too hard. She knocked him off his feet. He looked up at her with a gaping mouth and wide eyes. She drew her sword from its sheath.

"Evelyn!"

"Run, you damned fool!" yelled Evelyn, wild eyed. Her hands were beginning to visibly tremble.

The man staggered to his feet. Evelyn turned to join her companions. They were standing in a semi-circle facing out, weapons at the ready, uncertain as to where the attack was to come from.

"My lady——" the father yelled.

"Evelyn!"

Evelyn turned to face the father. Sweat was already on her forehead and upper lip.

"——the password," continued the man.

Another scream, this one dreadfully close. Evelyn felt her knees turn to gelatin. She kept her footing.

"They've seen us! Evelyn!"

"Let us be cleansed of this Rot," said Evelyn to the father, and she turned to join her companions. The man grabbed his children and ran East.

As Evelyn turned, she saw the hideous worm-like shape of the shambling horror in the darkness, its slithering, undulating motions bringing it closer to them. It was nearly a whole-man taller than the average person and thick. Behind the thing were an indiscernible number of others of the same blasphemous kin.

"We need to——" came the half-shaky voice of Evelyn, but it was cut off by the sudden whip of a tendril like appendage from out of the darkness. It made straight for Evelyn, but she rolled to one side of the attack. As she gained her feet again and went to charge in for a counter, she saw more tendrils swimming out of the darkness, toward her companions as the jaundiced, slimy skin of the unnameable thing came into the dim light. For half a moment she froze and felt a slight pang between her legs, and with it a faint, acrid smell. Her eyes suddenly stung. She caught her breath.

Miles dodged about like a mad acrobat, whilst Boone and Russell held their ground together, attacking the tentacle-like appendages of the inhuman horror, spilling its black blood upon the cobblestone. The blood had a strange, fungal scent to it, yet it had the consistency of thick mucus.

Barrett on the other hand, was not having so much luck. He was caught up in a number of the tendrils of a second creature who had reached the group of Reapers. He screamed in terror as they wrapped about him and squeezed and tore at his flesh. No matter how many times the massive Cabbage Reaper brought his mace down upon the worm-like flesh of the ghastly, charnel thing, it did little to halt its violence.

Evelyn cursed her momentary hesitation and rushed forward, heedless of all but Barrett and her desire to free him from the deadly clutches of the horrors in the darkness. Just as she reached it, dodging around two attacks from the strange being, and finding her sword did little but blunt damage to the corded-skin, a third creature reached its head—for so it could only be referred—out of the darkness. This time Evelyn felt a hot rush of liquid on her thighs as a thick, flat face, covered in eyes and lined with teeth crested out of the dark, and spit forth from its hideous maw a thick, black cloud of inky liquid. Then all went dark.

Evelyn reeled backwards, her eyes burning from the inky-substance. She dropped her sword, holding her face with both hands, as she cried out in pain. She was stumbling around in complete, pitch dark. She saw nothing and felt little else but the intense pain in her eyes. But she heard a confused cacophony of sounds.

Slashes, hacks, screeches, and horrors. She heard maddening inhuman cries from Barrett, and the sickening crush of bone and the rending of flesh. It was as though a chicken were being split open in full consciousness of the deed. With it came a hot spray on Evelyn's ear.

She heard the mad laughter of Miles, the silent monotony of the attacks of Russell and Boone, and the high-pitched screeches of the unnameable horrors. Somehow, she thought, the Reapers were able to score a solid blow.

A hot showering of thick, heavy goo splashed against Evelyn's left arm, weighing it down. She heard a gurgling sound and wheeled about, uncertain of what the sound and sensation pertained. She cursed and rubbed her eyes. She wanted to open them, to return to battle, to help her comrades.

Miles laughed again and again. Evelyn reeled in pain and from the throbbing sensation in her head. Then came a bone-chilling screech from impossibly inhuman lungs. Evelyn slipped on something wet. Her knee cracked against the stone pavement. She blinked. All black and more pain, and then something heavy clapped her shoulder.

"We need to run," came the silver-muffled voice of Boone.

Evelyn felt she could hardly stand, let alone run, but the sounds about her or lack thereof, told her that the tendrilled horrors had quitted that place—at least for the moment. She was on her feet with Boone's help and held onto him for support as best she could.

# VI

They ran for what felt like an endless stretch of miles, but Evelyn knew it couldn't have been very far. Her knee throbbed, and her head felt dizzy, as though it were bobbing in an endless sea. She lost her balance quite a few times during that blind dash to safety, but Boone held tightly to her. Her eyes still stung, but it was becoming more bearable. Her vision, however, was all uncertain shadowy shapes.

She heard the sounds of only one set of footfalls in front of her, and behind her came the faint screeches of the worm-like horrors from the dark.

Evelyn wanted nothing so much as to be far away from that place. She would even give her eyesight permanently for such a thing—though she'd gladly die if she could see Mavis just once more.

At length, Evelyn was carefully guided through a small space, with sliding, unstable footing, and guided to a spot where she was allowed to sit down. Her back rested against a cold, stable, stone wall. Vague, waving images danced before her vision, and the sounds around her faded in and out. A figure stood a distance away, standing before what might have been a hole in a wall, looking out into the dark night. Like everything else, the figure looked strangely mist-like, and the architecture of the room fell at impossible angles. Evelyn wondered if she did not dream.

A cool, gentle hand touched her forehead and then her cheek. Finally, it came to rest on her forearm. *Mavis.* She reached out and took the hand in hers. It was rough. Course. She sighed, and her whole body relaxed. *He had come.*

"That black ichor has gotten into her eyes," said Boone. He looked back at Evelyn. Her head swayed on her shoulders, like a branch in the wind. He let her hold onto his hand.

"Mavis..." the woman moaned.

"The path to Areglos is closed now," came a slightly high-pitched, scratchy voice. "There are too many of those things now, and we can't take them all at once."

*Was that...Russell's voice?* Evelyn was suddenly aware that she had never once heard Russell speak before. *But where was Miles?* Her head throbbed. She squeezed the hand she held. *At least Mavis is with me.* She could die happy right then and there.

"She might die," said Boone, "or worse. Those things were not here when we last came, and we've no idea what that black ichor does. She could change. Perhaps that's how it's done."

Russell sighed. He continued to look through the glassless window.

"We shouldn't have spread our ranks so thin."

Evelyn mused that it was such a strange voice for a redheaded man who carried a large hammer. She felt a hand wrapped around hers. *Whose hand is this?* She blinked. Her eyes stung, but the shapes of a long-abandoned building were coming into focus. She could see a caved in roof and a second floor. She saw that red-haired Russell stood looking out the lone standing window of the place. There was no door in or out, just a narrow path through the fallen rubble at the far end. She let go of the hand and blinked again.

"We'll just need to do it now," said Boone, taking his hand back.

"Pity," said Russell. "She is legendary, even among us. She would have been a great ally at least until we reached Areglos."

There was a pause.

"Be quick about it."

Evelyn looked up into the face of the owner of the hand. It was a silver mask, topped with a tricorn hat. Boone. Evelyn had never been this close to him before. She smelled a familiar scent over the frankincense which lined her own mask. It was a strangely calming scent, Boone's, but Evelyn could not quite place it over her own.

As Boone rose to his feet, Evelyn caught the sight of a strange necklace she had not noticed before. It dangled before her face only for a moment, but she noticed the strange rune fashioned in golden-copper, and it seemed as though the necklace were made of a fragment of old wood.

Russell continued to gaze through the window. Boone moved over and picked up something that was resting against the wall. When the moonlight hit it, just for a moment, Evelyn thought she noticed a glint of the same golden-copper colour as that on Boone's strange necklace.

*Lavender. That was the scent. Strange.*

The tall boots of Boone now stopped just in front of her. Evelyn reached out a hand, as she still needed help to steady herself. She felt standing would somehow help her out of the haze. *We need to get to Areglos.* She needed to get to Mavis.

"There are a few of them out there now," said Russell.

*That's fine. We could try running along the rooftops for a while.* Evelyn tried to push herself up, her hand still extended out for support. She couldn't understand why Boone was just watching her struggle and not helping her to stand.

There was a screech from outside. Those damnable things.

"I'm sorry, Evelyn," said Boone.

Evelyn looked up toward Boone, and she caught a golden-copper glimmer flickering in the moonlight as it sped toward her.

The female Reaper slipped to the side just in the nick of time as the curved sword fell with a clang into the stone wall. Leaning down on her elbow, Evelyn in one swift motion brought her knee to her chest and then with all her strength, pushing off the wall with her back, she thrust her foot forward. The bone-splitting snap told her she had hit her mark perfectly.

Boone fell forward with a gurgling grunt, and an acrid stench was notable over the aroma of frankincense and lavender. Then, using the wall to stead herself, Evelyn climbed to her feet, as Boone tried to scream over the choking bile as he lamented the ruin of his knee.

"Damn you, Boone. Do it quietly, I said!" said Russell, and he turned just as Boone had spit out sufficient chunks to cry out in pain. Evelyn was bending down to retrieve Boone's sword. There was a screech from outside.

"Oh, feck!" said Russell.

He reached for his great hammer which was laid beside the window, just as Evelyn grabbed the hilt of Boone's sword and brought it down upon the maimed-man's tricorn hat, spilling blood, and brains about the floor. Russell took two steps forward when a third screech, just behind him, made him turn and stiffen.

At the window, a gelatinous, jaundiced form swayed like seaweed in the ocean. Thick, corded tendrils shot from its body at the red-haired, hammer-wielding man. He screamed in terror as they wrapped about his legs, waist, and neck. Evelyn lept back against the wall in petrified disbelief, her eyes wide as she watched the scene play out.

With his free hands, Russell swung his hammer again and again, splashing black ichor into the air and upon the windowsill. Another screech was heard above the injured cries of Russell's foe, and just as Russell swung his hammer at the face of the blasphemous horror before him, sending it reeling back and breaking its grip upon him, the tendrils of a second horror made its way through the window, and this one was smart enough to reach for the man's arms first.

Russell swore, but it quickly died on his lips. Frustration turned to fear as more tendrils latched onto the man's body. The hammer fell to the floor with a clang. Then with a great pull of force, Russell shot through the window, his body snapping in half as he hit against the sill. Evelyn's stomach turned, and she choked back her sick with a burning sensation along her throat down to her chest.

Then followed a nauseating sound of crunching and slurping. Evelyn turned her head and tightly shut her eyes as though that would somehow stop her mind recreating what only her ears were witnessing. Her heart pounded in her chest. She felt a cool sweat steal over her skin. Then there was silence.

Evelyn opened her eyes. Her heart's pace began to settle, but still her head throbbed and her eyes ached. Breathing was difficult, but she was doing her best to steady and quiet it. It hurt to expand her chest and get the air down into her lungs—almost as though she were drowning. She took one last deep gulp of air and pulled down her mask.

Silence still, except for her almost imperceptible sighs and the throbbing of her heart and head. No other sounds cut the scene. The only movement was the shifting light of the moon behind the clouds, and the slow crawl of Russell's spilled viscera as gravity dragged it to the floor.

Evelyn waited longer still. She watched and studied

the darkness. She listened to the stillness. Nothing. Breathing slowly became easier, and she forced the air deep down into her lungs to help steady it despite the pain. Her heart still pounded, but slowly, less violent than before. Only, each pulse it sent forth caused her head to swim just a little.

The Reaper stepped forward, careful to plant her feet so that she didn't slip on the life Boone spilled upon the floor. Another step. Silence. A third step. Naught.

Evelyn had nearly reached the window and the hammer Russell left behind when suddenly part of the wall caved as an invertebrate horror crashed into the room. Tendrils swam about the air. The thing turned to Evelyn, its form mostly obscured by the shadows of the room and clouded sky, but the faint, dull moonlight shone through just enough for Evelyn to witness for a third time the blasphemous thing which slithered before her.

It turned quickly toward her; its countless black eyes fixed on her; its hideous, round maw undulating like the surface of a lake. She noted now its worm-like form, and the tendrils which grew along its underside, smaller toward the back, and growing longer and longer as they reached its head. Those tendrils, the longest of them, found purpose again and whipped out at the Reaper, but Evelyn equaled its speed. Only there were so many of those damnable appendages, and the weight of Boone's sword was perhaps a pound more than her own lost weapon—plenty enough to affect the speed and nature of her attacks. Evelyn was all about speed. Swift, dexterous movements had been one of the key things that separated Mavis's Church Reapers from the rest, save for those who Uncle Bram trained personally.

The horror whipped frantically in all directions, but always and ultimately toward Evelyn. More than once she was slapped by the snapping, cord-like appendages, and once a blow just missed her face when she dodged below it, sending her hat flying into the dark of the room. She was beginning to breathe heavily again. Her knee, swelling from the fall earlier, was further hindering her movements, as was the weight of the sword. But she had to wait for the right opening, lest the tendrils bring her to a definitive stop. Only, she knew that would soon happen if she did not strike a blow at last.

A number of tendrils just missed her as she slipped to one side of their oncoming insanity, and Evelyn planted her foot in order to pivot for a strike. Three of the creature's tendrils whipped back almost instantly, but Evelyn trusted and committed to her swing. With a smooth, crunching sound, the sword of Boone sliced straight through the oncoming tendrils, spraying black ichor into the air. Evelyn smiled despite herself.

The worm-like horror reeled backward as it screeched in pain, and Evelyn wasted no time. She rushed forward, sword held behind her for yet another blow, but her over-zealousness got the best of her. For as the creature reeled, the tendrils toward its lower end, shorter yet still long enough, shot out and grabbed hold of Evelyn's ankle. With a force she had never experienced before—even when Mavis trained her under the influence of his serum—the creature pulled and snapped its appendage so that Evelyn was thrown behind the thing. A table broke her fall, but the whiplash was sufficient to tear Boone's sword from her hand.

Evelyn coughed and grunted from the pain. She tried to stand, but her already bruised knee screamed with pain. She fell to her knees. It stung. She looked for the sword, but she caught a glimpse of Russell's hammer instead. Between her and the hammer was the unspeakable horror, the horror which now turned toward Evelyn, its tendrils—only three cut short—whipping chaotically once more. The eyes of the thing, though black and soulless, seemed to glare at Evelyn with murderous intent. The Reaper took a deep breath.

All as one, the creature's full set of tendrils whipped toward Evelyn, and as they hurtled toward her, the Reaper shifted all her weight to her uninjured leg. She pushed off, rolling just under the oncoming attack. She gained the hammer, and despite the immense pain, hoisted herself up onto her feet whilst lifting the hammer into the air. She grit her teeth against the sharp pain in her knee. It was all just enough to make the window of time before the hideous thing turned and sent its tentacled limbs against her again.

With crushing force, the hammer came down upon the eye-lined head of the unspeakable horror, and it caved in a visceral gush of thick, black ichor and unearthly pulp. The thing writhed, body and tendrils both whipping about in its death throes, its nerves still twitching despite the absence of a functioning brain. Evelyn might have been sick, hearing the wet slap of its body slowing on the floor, had her knee not been throbbing and her body not utterly exhausted.

She laid down on the floor, catching her breath and allowing her muscles to calm as she listened to the last pats of jaundiced, wormy flesh against the wooden planks. She closed her eyes and sighed.

She was alone now, but she had her duty to fulfill. It had been her plan, after all. She couldn't give up. She was the product of legendary Reapers: the niece of Bram, the pupil of Mavis. Mavis. She had to find him, if nothing else. She had to know what happened to him, what was so important in Oscar's letter that he had to leave them when they needed his guidance and knowledge most? When she needed him most.

Evelyn let out another sigh and struggled to her feet. She steadied herself, keeping her weight off the injured leg for the moment. That was going to slow her down, there was no doubt. She was going to have to do what she could to minimize the handicap. It was still a bit of a journey to Areglos, and she had no idea what she would come up against on the way, never mind what she would find inside the cathedral itself.

She sighed and looked about the room once more, working through a plan in her mind.

# VII

Once she got moving, the stiffness in Evelyn's leg began to ease. Even the pain dulled to a mild discomfort. She did her best to make certain the makeshift support she wrapped about her knee wasn't too restrictive. The wood was provided by the broken table, the cloth by Boone.

She made sure to keep the weight of both weapons on the side of her uninjured leg. They were of such a curious design, and though she found them a bit unwieldy, they were the only weapons she had—other than a single shot from the pistol strapped to her boot. What's more, she knew these two devices were effective against those blasphemous things. Both weapons had veins running through them of that same curious golden-copper substance as on Boone's necklace, and like Boone's wooden relic, both weapons had carved in them the same strange rune she had noted upon further inspection: the one that gave her the strange impression of a man being hung upside down, its arms forming a triangle in the air.

Given the condition of her leg, her fever dreamed idea of hopping along the rooftops nearly all the way to Areglos was out of the question. Fortunately, there were fewer and fewer of the infected the closer she came to Areglos and no sign whatever of the horrors. Though she occasionally heard their cries off in the distance.

Slowly and methodically, Evelyn cut a stealthy path from the hovel where Boone's naked ruin lay to the bridge connecting Kirklyn's Northern Quarter to the patch of land owned by the Church of Areglos. She was aided in her cloak-and-dagger journey by the shadows cast by the large buildings of the city, enhanced by the cloud-covered moon. Not a single infected noticed her, and she thanked her luck that she was able to conserve her energy for whatever battle lay ahead.

Though the horrors did not appear to her again, and though she saw fewer of the infected, living or dead, the aspect of the city only grew more nightmarish as she traveled the shadows of its moss-cloaked masonry.

The once white bricks of the City, blue in the moonlight, now had corrupted to a dark, muddy grey, and the mortar between was so mossed, it looked as though the City's architects had employed the stuff during its inception. Whole houses and parts of business were caked in moss, so that they too looked more like natural forms of the landscape, rather than unnatural corruptions. And then there was the air.

Glistening in the sky like moonlit snowflakes was the light flurry of glowing spores, pale green and blue. They fell around Evelyn as she picked her way along the uneven path, and she thanked her luck that she still had her mask. Yet even with the protection, the air felt choking and stifling about her—as though she were drowning in its moisture. The spore-like substance was familiar to her, as it fell in places where the Rot was thickest, but only lightly, like fireflies in a dark, summer field. Now, here in the Northern Quarter, the spores fell thicker than she had ever before seen them.

She wondered why Uncle Bram had never seemed particularly interested in the spores. His obsession was the strange serum the Church had given the Shields in their early days. It was the old communion of the Shields of the Church which had given them their unnatural speed and ability, making them quite adept at fighting the plague which had come to Stowshaw, and later the Rotten Lunatics of Kirklyn. But when the Shields became Reapers and trained a new generation of acolytes, the serum was only given to their own Church

Reapers who had been Shields of the Church. Uncle Bram was convinced it was the source of the strange sickness that ailed all the former-Shields who had left the Church of Areglos. That was before the Curse took him and things grew ever more dire in Kirklyn.

Few of the now living Reapers had ever tasted of it. Mavis was one, perhaps the only one left besides Oscar, and he had forbidden Evelyn even once to taste of it, despite his own dependence on it. That he even possessed vials of the stuff, Evelyn may have been the only person to know, and that secret she would never tell. With the death of Bram, the serum had become almost a thing of legend.

The thought of Mavis brought her back to the present, and she looked through the falling spores and rotten homes to the growing menace of the cathedral before her—or at least what she had formerly known to have been the Cathedral her whole life before that moment.

# VIII

Evelyn had come to the end of the thinning stone forest of Kirklyn's businesses and residences, and before her ran the wide stone bridge which ended at the courtyard of the Grand Cathedral of the Church of Areglos. It had been six months since Mavis went there to see Oscar, six months since he left the care of the Church Reapers to Evelyn, six months since she last looked upon his hard, weather-beaten face.

For a moment she hesitated, remembering the remaining untainted citizens and the ten men she left behind to protect them in the Eastern Quarter. Those nameless, tentacled things roamed the city somewhere; horrors which few believed truly existed—even among the Reapers who had already seen so much in the time since the Lunatic Rot's outbreak. How would they fare against such mind-numbing horrors? But even as the thoughts came to her, the moon peeked out from behind the clouds, and Evelyn saw the rotting corpse of the once great cathedral.

Few spots of it now shewed the gleaming virgin white it had once been before the horrible Rot had tainted the city of Kirklyn—long before the arrival of those unspeakable horrors. Vines and moss grew all about the stone work, though unlike the architecture of Kirklyn, the growing Rot seemed almost to support the falling structure, rather than consume it. To look upon it, one might make a loose connection to a cocoon of some-sort. Bits of masonry struck out from the encroaching growth, sometimes at angles impossible to be made by the hands of Man.

The Rot spread out from the cathedral and halfway across the bridge. It had already taken much of the physical stone of Kirklyn to varying degrees, as much as it had its people, but here the Rot seemed concentrated. Only the Western Quarter looked as completely infected. The sight instantly pulled at Evelyn's heartstrings. Whatever was happening here, she could not leave Mavis to such an unknown and horrifying fate.

Evelyn stepped out from the shadows of the last

buildings before the bridge and into the cold, pale light of the moon. Suddenly, an inhuman cry went out from the distant bridge to Areglos—a cry not like the horrors of before, precisely, for there was a tinge of humanity in its timbre.

Evelyn looked ahead and saw two figures rise from the moss-covered bridge, half-camouflaged by the myriad of foetid colours—both the colours of the moss on the bridge and of the figures themselves. They were anthropomorphic in nature, almost human, though whatever humanity had been there before now was gone. Their forms were twisted into impossible shapes, with a swollen head possessing eight eyes and a stretched, twisted mouth full of many-pointed fangs. Their arms had grown in length, though not so much in girth, so that they looked as though their appendages had been stretched on a rack without breaking. Their legs, by comparison, were stunted, though not much shorter than that of the men they once were. Though their feet had lengthened, creating the spring-like bend of a wolf's hind paws—or those of a cat. There was a curve to their spines, and from them, in a line, grew short tentacles, similar but not quite like the tendrils of the horrors she and her lost allies had met but hours before. Their chests and neck seemed swollen as well, thick with sinew and bone, and from their rounded shoulders there seemed to grow a pair of short, bat-like wings, and their hair looked now like a twist of thorny horns.

They both walked with a hollow, shambling gait, and as yet, they had not taken notice of Evelyn, even as she drew slowly closer to the bridge and the horror of these things came more and more into view. As she slowly drew closer, Evelyn could see that some clothing still clung to the half-human forms, and that garb was similar to those church men depicted in the statue at the center of Kirklyn. Though these living specimens were a great deal more horrifying by the extreme nature of their deformities and the fact that they walked and breathed with life.

Each of the half-humans carried a crude, cross-shaped weapon in whichever hand was least effected by the metamorphosis. Evelyn could not have identified who the two men had been, but the sight of them made her whole body pulse with petrifying electricity. She feared for Mavis all the more. With her free hand, she took Boone's oddly curved, golden-copper blade from where it hung from her belt. Her opposite hand gripped tightly to Russell's weighty hammer. She swallowed back her fear, and with a cold, determined countenance, Evelyn slowly continued forward to meet the two half-human creatures. Though picking her way as silently as she could, the movement and proximity of Evelyn caught the attention of the one of the two creatures. It let out another inhuman, bestial cry, it's eyes widening with lunacy, and its comrade marked the oncoming Reaper as well. Both fiends rushed toward her like two rabies-crazed hounds, as Evelyn's boots scraped along the ground as she moved to meet them with her determined yet injured gait.

She could see the hollow, lunatic gleam in the many-eyed skulls of the oncoming creatures, bestial and otherworldly, and by all accounts completely insane.

As the two once-men approached the Reaper, they hesitated for a moment, and a strange, unconscious recognition shewed in their eyes. Not for Evelyn—no—but for the rune-carved, golden-copper veined weapons that Evelyn held in each hand. She noted this, and gripped all the more confidently upon them, as the two maddened church men continued toward their prey.

Doing her best not to telegraph her movements, Evelyn shifted her weight to her back leg ever so imperceptibly, and she raised her sword-arm in front of her with false intent. The creatures were nearly upon her now. The hammer was undoubtedly the clumsier of the two weapons for Evelyn, and so she hoped the slight feint would be distraction enough. One of the crazed fiends let out another howl.

Evelyn tightened her jaw. *Almost there.* They raised their weapons. She could see the steam of their breath in the cool night air. She slowly inhaled. Now.

Deciding in a moment on the more deformed of the two, Evelyn swung the hammer up and over her head with all the strength she had. Such a large commitment at the outset was a risk, but she was trusting to the momentum of the creatures and her feint to work to her advantage. With all the force, momentum, and use of gravity she could muster, Evelyn brought the hammer down toward the half-deformed creature. It came down with such force that Evelyn felt the impact through her entire arm as it smashed and chipped the brick pavement with a loud crash.

Evelyn took in a hissing breath, but before she could even attempt to retrieve the hammer from the stone ground, the second creature was upon her. It came in with such speed and force that she hadn't a second to dodge. *Too fast.* Nothing like she would have expected. Evelyn brought up her sword to meet the creature's crossed weapon just in the nick of time, but under the force of the blow, she slid backward, dragging the hammer a few inches as she did.

Such speed, such power, Evelyn had never before experienced, even in her spars with Mavis, when he came at her with all his inhuman abilities that she might be prepared for such equally inhuman foes. Could this be what Uncle Bram was always speaking about? Mavis would never answer her inquiries on the matter, but once or twice she had secretly observed him injecting himself with a modest amount of the reddish-black substance. Mavis! She had to find him.

The two crazed fiends attacked with reckless abandon, but so inhuman was their speed and strength that even Evelyn's sharp and precise techniques counted for little—and she was yet getting used to the handicap of her unfamiliar load out. She rarely swung the hammer, rather using the weight of it to propel herself swiftly between the two relentless foes. Only when the timing was right would she swing the thing up and downward again, hoping for a blow that would never gain purchase, but using the momentum to propel herself faster into the next attack. It was an unorthodox style for her, but she had seen other Reapers apply similar techniques.

The sword quickly became her preferred tool, but too often she needed to deflect a killing strike from one of the creatures, as she simultaneously ducked or dodged the attack of the other. She rarely was on the offensive, and when she attempted such, it often led to near-dire consequences, leaving her open to an attack from the one she was not at that moment attacking. Twice those cross-shaped blades nearly ended Evelyn's life for true, and the gashes on her arms, the two on her leg, and the one tear in her shoulder told the tale of those blows she couldn't quite escape as she might have otherwise done with ease against those infected by the Lunatic Rot.

Her seeping wounds were draining her strength as much as the use of those weighted weapons. Then there was her knee, beginning to swell and throb once more. Evelyn knew she could not keep up such a pace forever, even as agile, and capable as she was. If she did not do something fast, she was going to die there. She needed to live. She needed to end the nightmare. She needed to find Mavis. And at the thought of Mavis, she remembered the small pistol attached to her boot. It was that or nothing.

A slash from one of the cross-shaped blades sliced into her left shoulder blade, and she cried out in pain. The wound was not mortal, but it was enough to send her to her knee—*that* knee. The price for thinking in the midst of combat. She brought her blade up to meet that of one of the creatures, narrowly rolling away from an attack from the other, keeping her hand on the hammer as she did. It was a risk, but she was going to have to pull it off or die.

Like a serpent, she struck out at the last attacking maniac with the curved sword, and she used the momentum to rise to her feet and swing the hammer back toward the other creature as it came in. The thing dodged backward as Evelyn hoped it might. She turned back upon the creature behind her and parried a blow with her sword and swiftly countered with a strike. The thing dodged, but Evelyn had not over-committed. Again, she used the momentum of springing back toward the second creature to swing the hammer again. She felt the wound in her back tearing, and involuntarily grit her teeth and winced. Not good. That momentary hiccup allowed the thing to slip the hammer-blow even more easily than the first. She couldn't slow down yet. She had to hold out just a bit longer.

Again, the half-human that was behind her closed in, and again Evelyn parried and countered. But Evelyn made for a second strike, just as the other creature slipped to one side and toward Evelyn, no doubt anticipating she would swing the hammer for a third time. The instincts of that bestial brain were correct. Evelyn was already lifting the hammer as it came in to finish her off.

The cross-shaped weapon sped downward with deadly accuracy, but Evelyn swung the hammer differently on the third strike. Rather than above her head and downward, she swung it in an upward arc, toward the oncoming creature. The thing acted quickly, but so committed was it that the hammer clipped it as the weapon made its way upward. Evelyn held fast for a little longer as the hammer was brought upward and then arching downward again at the oncoming creature. About a foot before it connected with the stone floor of the bridge, Evelyn let go of the hammer. It was just enough of a window.

She turned and ducked down as she sped in toward the creature who had been clipped slightly by the hammer's upward swing. The creature slashed at her, but missed, and as Evelyn rose, she grabbed the pistol from her boot, cocked it, and aimed at the creature's face point-blank. She did not know if the weapon would do any damage to the inhuman thing, but that was not her plan. The creature howled and staggered backward, as the blast went off. Its hands went up, too late, to cover its face, and that's when Evelyn stabbed forward and drove the curved blade home.

Blackish-red ichor sprayed from the wound as Evelyn just as swiftly pulled the sword back through the creature's chest. She turned backward to the second foe, as the first fell forward with a dull, wet sound against the stone. She brought her pistol up to deflect the others' oncoming attack. It barely did the job.

The blow missed Evelyn, but the gun was torn from her hand with such force that she too was thrown to the ground in her effort to keep her grip on the spent weapon. The force of the attack hurt, but she couldn't stop now.

She rolled with the momentum which had sent her to the ground and gained her feet again, though her muscles were beginning to cramp and ache. The creature was on her again with another strike. She ducked it. And another. She slipped to one side. She began to swing her sword for a counter, but a third strike from the mad creature came with such speed that she had to change the angle of the sword and block the attack. She planted a foot behind her, and something rounded hit her right on the instep, and her foot began to slide.

The blow connected with her sword as her foot slid on the fallen pistol beneath her feet. The two combined sent Evelyn backward onto her back with a crashing thud. The wind shot out of her lungs, and she gasped to get air back into them. Her head rung. The maddened creature, encouraged by this fortunate turn, wasted no time in finishing the battle.

Before Evelyn could draw a full breath into her lungs, the creature brought its cross-shaped weapon down upon her. She brought her sword up to meet it, and the unholy weapon crashed down with such force that the sword nearly bounced back into Evelyn's face. So it was with the second and the third and the fourth attacks. The fifth bounced her sword backward, and Evelyn only narrowly moved her head before the sword smashed back into the stone ground.

The sword quivered in her hand, and she hadn't the strength to raise it when a sixth attack came down upon her. She rolled to the side of it and up onto her knees, but the creature was so fast. It turned its sword and swung it in an arc, with such force that Evelyn was knocked back onto her backside.

When the next blow came, she used her free hand to help support her block and placed it near the tip of the sword. She turned and brought the hilt against the creature's crossed-blade and forcefully guided it down to the stone floor. Then she swiftly brought the blade back and slashed at the creature's face, as she rose back onto her knee. The maddened creature lept back, giving Evelyn just enough room to rise to her feet. She rushed toward her retreating foe, noting that the hammer lay just beyond it.

The creature changed the direction of its attack, and aimed low. Evelyn lept over the attack and rolled to momentary safety. She knew the thing would only be a half-second behind her. It seemed not even to tire. With all the speed she could muster, and ignoring the sharp pain in her knee, Evelyn sprinted toward the hammer and ducked to grab its handle. Using the momentum of her run, she ran around the hammer's head, gripping the handle all the while, and when she came around, hoisted it into the air. The insane creature was nearly upon her and quickly dodged around Evelyn just as the hammer began its descent downward. There was no way the heavy, ponderous thing was going to hit its mark, and the thing was going to be behind her before Evelyn had finished the strike—but that had been her plan.

Just as Evelyn brought the hammer up into the air, she raised the sword in her other hand, keeping it at an angle behind her, and out of sight of the insane creature. She spun the hammer around and down, while bringing the sword in the same arc, only opposite the hammer. So, when the creature dashed around the great hammer, it was met with the unseen, oncoming saw—and it only came to realise its error a second too late.

With all her strength and speed Evelyn pulled the sword through. With a spray of foetid viscera, the head of the creature, followed by its body, smacked with a wet slap against the stone floor, and Evelyn followed.

# IX

Like luminescent jellyfish, the spores floated and bounced about the air, glinting against the moonlight above. A rushing sound drowned out all else, and there was a sense of throbbing as each little light swelled and dissipated in the deep ocean of the night. A chill ran through as calm rushed over all. There was no intake of breath, and vision began to blur.

Then Evelyn let out a sigh.

Despite the pain and stiffness of her muscles, further intensified by the frigid and unforgiving stone beneath her, Evelyn lay there, staring up at the pale moon, allowing her heart and her breath to steady once more. Her head ached, and her knee felt tight and stiff. As soon as her breath was caught, she struggled to her feet and began to work and bend the stiffened joint. She reached down to retrieve Boone's sword, though she left Russell's hammer. It would be too difficult to wield now, and though she knew not what lie ahead of her, her only hope was that there were no more of those insane creatures.

*Mavis.* She thought again of Mavis.

Evelyn looked up at the Cathedral. It was just far enough away that the short walk would allow the blood to flow back into her muscles and to give them enough time to rest before the next stage. Slowly at first, the crescent-curved sword sheathed at her hip, Evelyn limped forward along the bridge toward the once-shining bronze doors of the Grand Cathedral of Areglos. With each step, a sharp pain ran through her knee, but the stiffness began to break. The cold, sea-like air cooled her, as it brushed against her sweat-damped skin, and the movement of her joints helped warm the injured knee. Her muscles were sore, tired, but she was not yet at the point of collapse. She would have to keep moving so as not to let the cold stiffness set in again.

By the time she reached the doors of the chapel, the limp was barely notable, and the heavy breath she drew in was not from her aches, but rather the shock of how much even the bronze doors had changed with the Rot. It had not been so long ago that the doors stood in all their cast-beauty, as untainted and gleaming as the day they were hung—long before Evelyn was born. Now they stood green and white from the heavy moisture of the air. Not even the bronze doors had been saved from the Rot, and with one last jolt of pain, she thought of Mavis. A cold sweat beaded the back of her neck. But Evelyn sighed out the pain, just as Mavis had taught her, and she leaned forward.

With both hands, she pushed on the double doors of the Grand Cathedral of Areglos, and the doors rumbled and creaked against her touch. But the sound was barely audible, for as if in answer to her arrival, from the towers above rang the hollow, resonant bells of Areglos. It was the first time in over a month that she had heard their sound.

# X

Upon opening the door, Evelyn was met with the once-glorious sight of the now decaying hall of the Grand Cathedral. Its mix of white and gold now stained by the green-black rot which had come to infect the city of Kirklyn so wholly. Foetid fungus grew up the colonnade; moss covered half the stone floor. From the ceiling hung lichen as if they were chandeliers, and the pews were half fallen to the Rot. Yet for all of this, and the memories which Evelyn had of the place in its glory, the Reaper had eyes only for the dais and the shape upon it.

There, as though in prayer, a man knelt upon the ground, as still as though he were a statue carved in resemblance of a man. He wore a long coat and tall boots, both of which looked worn and tattered. A hat lay on the ground beside him, looking hardly newer than the rest of his accouterments, and its absence from the man's head revealed a nearly greyed, longish shock of hair, which thinned in a circular fashion toward the back top of the head. Evelyn knew that hair. She knew that balding spot intimately. She knew those clothes, too, in their better days.

"Mavis," she called, but her voice was hoarse. She choked back tears. She swallowed hard and took a deep breath. Her hands were shaking.

"Mavis!" she cried again, and this time the head of the man kneeling upon the dais twitched at the sound of her voice.

A goblet fell to the floor beside the man with a clunk, and from it spilled the half-finished black-red contents. With its now emptied hands, it picked up its hat and placed it atop its head. Then, slowly, the figure began to rise. It hardly made a sound as it did, but for a slight creaking so quiet, Evelyn was barely certain she heard. As it rose, it took from the floor a sickle and a blunderbuss which she had not noticed beforehand. Then, fully risen, the thing slowly began to turn, and Evelyn choked back tears for a second time.

The face, that face which Evelyn knew so well, had the familiar grey stubble all about its chin, and its nose was the same flattish shape. The wrinkles around the eyes were just as they had always been. Yet those eyes. Those horrible eyes locked upon Evelyn without the slightest hint of recognition, and they were stretched and swollen—like the eyes of a creature of the deep sea. There was no glint of sane thought behind them—only seeming hollow and hateful—as crazed as the two things she had fought on the bridge. And like the eyes of those fungoid half-humans, the eyes which now glared at Evelyn seemed almost to glow with a reddish hue.

The thing which stood before her now was not quite as deformed as the creatures upon the bridge, but there was a scaly rot which grew upon its otherwise human skin. Evelyn saw that the greying hair seemed to twitch and curl like tentacles dangling on either side of the still recognisable face of Mavis. Then Evelyn noticed for the first time how those once strong yet gentle calloused hands now resembled claws, and how the limbs attached to those claws twisted and bulged in ways that were sickeningly inhuman. The thing opened wide its mouth and let out a horrible, insane cry, and Evelyn noted the yellowed, fang-like teeth that circled in two rows inside of the once-man's mouth.

Tears rolled down Evelyn's cheeks, all her efforts to stop them for naught. She felt her legs weaken and she nearly fell to her knees, but the thing that had once been Mavis came forward, increasing its speed as it did. Evelyn felt her stomach turn, and she squinted her eyes against her tears. She tightened her grip upon the hilt of Boone's sword, and her legs found their strength again. She wiped her eyes with the back of her free hand.

Mavis was on her in no time. He moved fast, faster even than the two upon the bridge. Hardly surprising. Mavis had been the first Church Reaper. All who came after had learned from him—even Uncle Bram. Yet Evelyn had never seen Mavis like this. He seemed almost to disappear momentarily when he moved. He was strong—so strong. Stronger and faster than any spar they had before, and Mavis had never held back with his best pupil.

Evelyn could do little else but move about just out of Mavis's range, blocking his attacks only when they fell just right or she was too slow to act. But even the blocks were barely executed in time, and more than once Evelyn nearly met her end in the flurry of blows which were unleashed upon her.

Tears streamed down her cheeks again as she squinted through wet lashes to look into the wild-mad face of her once-mentor. So good had been her training by him, she could not have stopped herself from defending herself if she tried. It was instinctive. Yet she never once went on the offensive.

"Please, Mavis. It's Evelyn. Please," the woman cried, her voice cracking. "I came for you."

But Mavis, or what once had been the man, seemed not to hear her words. He continued on in a half-mad way, hacking and slashing at his former pupil with deadly precision.

Evelyn's knee began to ache yet again. She knew it would not hold forever. She had pushed herself too hard. But what other choice had she? She begged and pleaded with Mavis, even professing how tired she was becoming, but the blood-crazed Reaper continued his onslaught.

"Mavis," she whispered one last time. "Please."

But if Mavis heard her, he showed no sign of it, and Evelyn felt that her knee was about to buckle beneath her. Her blocks were becoming dangerously slower. She looked into those blood-red eyes, at the grey stubble that surrounded those gritted fangs. No. This was not Mavis.

With what strength was left to her, Evelyn brought her sword up as another blow from the Reaper's sickle spun toward her. This time she wrapped her other hand around the sword's tip, and with both hands drove the cross-guard down into the curve of the sickle. Metal caught upon metal, and Evelyn forced the two curved weapons down to the floor. Then with one swift motion, she let go of the sword tip, brought her foot down upon the sickle's blade, and raised the sword above her head for a killing blow. It happened so fast.

Mavis lept back from the oncoming blow, even as Evelyn began to bring it down, letting sickle fall beneath Evelyn's foot. There was a loud, thunderous crack, and Evelyn stumbled back, pain seared through her body at various points in her stomach, chest, arms, and legs. She held onto her sword as tightly as she could, but her legs gave out almost instantly. With that she wretched, and a warm flow of acrid, stinging fluids ran down her thighs. Her vision began to blur.

The thing that was formerly Mavis let out an inhuman, savage cry. Evelyn's head was lolling on her neck. She couldn't die here. Mavis threw his emptied blunderbuss to the side and rushed forward, stooping as he went to pick up his fallen sickle.

She had to save Mavis.

He was nearly upon her.

*Mavis.*

He pulled back the sickle behind him.

*No.*

He began to bring the sickle across his body, aimed with deadly precision toward Evelyn's neck.

With all her last strength, Evelyn swung the strange, runed sword. With little effort it shore through Mavis's thigh just above the knee. The oncoming blow fell limply, though Evelyn would not have been there to feel it. She crumpled to the floor, lying upon her side, shivering with pain.

# XI

She could not have long been out of consciousness. Perhaps only seconds. Blood still poured freshly from the open wound where had once been the creature's leg. Warm, black-red blood. She was losing blood, too. Her vision fogged. She needed blood.

"Evelyn."

Evelyn opened her eyes. Her vision clearing for a moment. She looked over toward the speaker of that voice. That familiar voice. She knew that face, and despite the pain in her frigid limbs—all over her body—she smiled.

"Evelyn. Please."

*Yes, Mavis? I'll do anything for you.*

She feebly propped herself up onto her elbow. The pain in her stomach and chest was excruciating. Her stomach turned. Bits of the last meal she'd eaten earlier that day fell upon the floor beneath her, tinged with a reddish hue. She gave it little thought. The wound in Mavis's leg was so terrible.

*Where was his leg? Would he ever walk again?*

Tears began to well in her eyes. She had to save Mavis. Despite the pain in her body, she slowly dragged herself the short distance between them, her stomach turning once more. She swallowed back the bile. It burned her throat, making the desire to wretch even greater.

"Please, Evelyn. It has to be you."

With a shaking hand, Mavis reached out to grab a sword which had fallen near him. Evelyn blinked. It shone with a goldish-copper colour in the faint light of the Cathedral, and she thought she could discern runes upon it. Strange runes. What did they mean? Mavis slowly lifted the sword and held it out toward Evelyn.

"Please. It has to be you, Evelyn. I'm so sorry."

She had reached Mavis, ignoring the sword.

*Sorry?*

The shot.

*No, Mavis. It's okay. You're sick. You couldn't control it. But look. You're better now. I saved you.*

She turned and with half closed eyes she looked upon the pulsating ruin that had been Mavis's leg. *Oh, Mavis. I'll save you.*

She needed blood. Her vision fogged. She swayed. She reached out for balance. Her hand closed around a thick, iron bar. It felt heavy in her hand. She blinked. Her vision began to clear again. *Mavis. He looked so handsome. So tired.* She smiled, tears welling in her eyes. She saw his eyes glistened too. He smiled. Her heart ached. She leaned forward to embrace him. She fell forward, her vision failing her.

# XII

Hollow rang the resonant bells of the Church of Areglos. It had been so long since Evelyn had last heard their dissonant lament. It was soothing to hear them once more, and she wondered what the time of day was. *How many times had the bells rung?*

She opened her eyes. Her vision was hazy. Beneath her she felt the broad, muscular chest of Mavis. She sighed and smiled. Her head swam. *I'm not ready to get up yet, whatever time it is. It's too seldom the time we get together. I could lay with him forever.*

Her whole body ached. It must have been a hard day of training. Mavis wouldn't mind then if they stayed in bed just a little longer. Darkness nearly took her again.

She blinked and blinked again. Then her stomach turned.

From Mavis's midsection like a headstone stood the strange, curved, runic sword that she had taken from Boone. Black-red blood oozed from the wound, and Evelyn felt her veins pulse as she watched wide-eyed its enticing flow. She turned away, tears already stinging her eyes, and looked into the cold, hollowed face of Mavis. It was stiff and sightless, yet he looked more like himself than he had during their battle. Evelyn fell forward. Tears blinded her sight. She shut them tight against their stinging flow. She gritted her teeth, and her body began to heave up and down as she buried her face in Mavis's ice-cold neck.

As her body twitched, pain raced through it, and Evelyn's weeping was cut short as an acrid burn raced up from her stomach. She coughed out a fresh flow of sick. Red ran the liquid over Mavis's chest, and Evelyn swooned. Her eyes became heavy, and her body began to grow cold. More than once she nearly fell over for the last time.

As her head lolled and darkness slowly took her, Evelyn again looked at the warm flow of black-red from Mavis's wound. Her veins pulsed again. Her eyes became just a little clearer. Whatever it was, it seemed to flow with life, even as Mavis lay lifeless.

Evelyn reached out a feeble, shaking hand. It was warm to the touch—hot almost—and she was so, so cold. *Mavis.* Her head reeled again. Her veins throbbed in her temples as all feeling left her legs. *We can be together.*

The smell of the black-red stuff seemed almost sweet by what little sense of smell she had left. *The blood. Mavis's blood. Mavis's life.* They could still have a life together. They could still be one.

Evelyn felt her consciousness begin to fade. She coughed up more of her own red-life. She leaned toward the open wound.

*Mavis. His life. Together again. Oh, Mavis.*

The serum. She recalled Uncle Bram's words. His Curse.

Evelyn placed her mouth upon the wound. The black-red ooze was so warm, and she was so cold. Life. Mavis's life.

They would be together, again.

*Forever.*

# Dashiell

**I**

ollow rang the resonant bells of the Church of Areglos, but who would hear them? The city of Kirklyn looked like a rotting corpse from his view from the balcony atop the Grand Cathedral. This was not the greatness and holy boon they were promised. This was not a fulfillment of the visions the Great One had given them. Here before him was the price of Bishop Mallory's greed and his followers' unquestioning loyalty to him. Mallory was weak to have followed a similar path to that of Vicar Orianna. They already knew the dangers of sin against the Great One and the price it cost the people of Stowshaw. Had he not doubts about Mallory? But it was not until the changes began to occur that he removed himself from the Inner Circle. He felt his shin begin to writhe. *Was it too late for to repent? Was it too late for those who saw the signs and removed themselves early?*

"Deacon Dashiell," came the voice of a young priest who had just stepped out onto the balcony.

Dashiell turned his cold eyes from the city. He was a tall, thin, and somber-looking man. Not a hair dotted his cleft chin, but wrinkles fell like ribbons along his high cheekbones. His crown was like a mountain surrounded by clouds. He did not smile at the arrival of the young priest, but eyed him with half-closed, intelligent eyes.

"Who was slain?" said Deacon Dashiell in the drawn, thin, yet deep voice he commanded with; the voice which had echoed so many times through the colonnade of the Grand Cathedral to the glory of Kirklyn's masses.

"Mavis fell to the intruder," answered the young priest.

*Mavis. He was so unfit for the job. A fine Reaper, yes, but Oscar had never once complained quite so much as Mavis did—not until the end, when the transformation had finally taken hold.* But those men were of Mallory's crew. Gervaise had never complained, but that was to be expected. It was as much his discovery as it was Mallory's. And Mortimer? Well, rumours were he had become as blood-drunk as the Twins and all the other lessers after him, hardly sentient to anything but their duty. It was Orianna's gluttony that caused Mortimer's change, and it was evident that Mallory too had long ago succumbed to such sinful ways himself and in his avarice had left the others yearning for the Holy Visions and the Eldritch Knowledge.

"She," said the young priest, "carried a strange weapon. It has weird runes upon it and a golden-copper sheen when the light hits it right. The sight of it seemed to repel the others."

Dashiell turned his glance toward the South. He looked into the distant night, well beyond moon and the glittering fall of spores. *Dayton.*

Fitting that the name came to him just then. It had

all begun with the Great Schism and Dayton's discovery. Now Dashiell was to lead a schism of his own. Only this was not in rebellion and fear of greatness, as had been Dayton's great failure, but rather the reclaiming of greatness from those who were unfit to be the custodians of their god. Just look at what the city had become because of Mallory's greed.

"We can look into the matter later, Julian" said Deacon Dashiell at length. "We'll need to be done ere the creatures return from their hunt." Dashiell turned his cold eyes upon the young man again.

"How long has it been since they set out?"

"About an hour or so ere the intruder's arrival," said the young priest.

Dashiell did naught but nod in affirmation, though in his mind again he mused about how perfectly it all seemed to be falling into place. Fate through faith. Now this intruder would be no usurper at all. How fitting that a new Guardian be made on the very night that Bishop Mallory was to be thrown from his seat. Perhaps it was fate, or the very will of the Great One. If only he could know for certain. If only the horded greed of Mallory's Inner Circle had not kept the visions from he and the others—and just when Dashiell believed he was beginning to truly understand the will of the Great One.

At that thought, another spasm ran through Dashiell's leg and almost up to his hip. His blood ran cold. He caught onto the banister of the balcony, effectively hiding the physical change from the young priest. So many of them had succumbed to it: the physical withdrawals of the Great One's communion—

communion taken in excess under the foolish tutelage of Mallory. If Dashiell was to lead what few remained, he could not shew weakness of any kind.

Though if the young priest at all had grown suspicious of or even concerned for the veteran priest, Dashiell was saved this—though not by any bell.

A faint, though blood-chilling scream echoed from the East, and followed by it came others of like kind. The spasms in Dashiell's hip began to subside.

*There isn't a moment to lose.*

Spurred to action by the screams from the East, Dashiell turned from the balcony and marched into the cathedral. The young priest followed hurriedly behind him, a bit of moisture shewing on his forehead, though otherwise the youth seemed as determined and driven forward as the man who led them.

# II

With a few strides of his long shanks, Dashiell came down the hall and into an open, circular area of the upper cathedral. There, it seemed strangely enough, the Rot and fungoid growths had not touched the alabaster walls of the Grand Cathedral. Candles sat in sconces upon the decorative columns that rose at regular intervals along the walls, though there was an odd paleness to their flames, as though the air itself choked their light; however, there was not otherwise any visible sight of fog.

In the center of the chamber stood six other

deacons of the Church of Areglos, all robed in the finery which their position had dictated was their right to adorn. Each man, both young and old—though none so young as the youth which had come to retrieve Dashiell—looked at their chosen leader with the stern, immovable expressions that years of sermons had helped them to practice. Dashiell could see in their eyes the fear and uncertainty and even the anger they felt inside. Dashiell did not judge them on this point, for they were not warrior Reapers, but rather men of the cloth, however deep their fervour—and for these men that fervour did indeed run deep—all but for one, that is.

"Where is Deacon Clay?" spoke Dashiell, his voice, like the candles, seeming thin and obscured.

"He was taken to the sick ward," spoke Deacon Crossley from the small congregation. "It'll be like the others. He began screaming insanities ere we had strapped him to his bed. Death cannot be long off for Clay."

"We'll all soon go the same way," said Deacon Uzziah. "We should have moved sooner, long before it came to this."

"Spending any more time on this will only have us miss another opportunity," said Deacon William. "We're moving now. I doubt any of us could have seen what was happening sooner than we did. We all had to recognise what was happening in our own time. We should thank the Great One that our visions remained clear enough. Others were not so fortunate."

Many of them, like Dashiell, had been members of the Inner Circle, and those who had been, knew well their history and the truths known only to that higher order. They recognised the signs of sinful avarice when they began to shew: the slow, painful metamorphosis of flesh and bone. Perhaps the others noticed these signs, but they traded their piety for sin, hoping they would not be cursed for it the same as Orianna and Mortimer. Perhaps those who remained among Bishop Mallory's chosen ranks believed the Great One had other motivations for the curse it laid on Stowshaw.

*What do you believe now, Mallory, of what you have become?*

Again, Dashiell felt a tickle in his hip, as though the very bones of his body were momentarily losing their firmness and writhed tentacle-like beneath his skin. Dashiell was determined not to succumb. He would not die as Clay and the others who went before, and he would not become as one of Mallory and his followers. Now was the time, whilst they were away and they could freely gain access to the Great One, unguarded by those hideous creatures. How they would deal with those things afterward, Dashiell put his faith in the Great One to sort that out. First, they needed to rescue their glorious god, just as the Church Shields had once done in Stowshaw, only this time It would not be placed in the hands of a madman. It would be safe, cared for, and unabused.

Without a word further, Deacon Campbell, produced a few torches, and two long candle sticks, formerly used in various rites and processions performed by the Church of Areglos ere the coming of the Great One. Before they had traded one invisible god for a tangible and infinitely more capable one. The torches were given out, one to each of the men present, including Dashiell. These they lit using the flames of the candles about the hall, and such as those candles, despite the full blaze of their flame, the priest's lights burned pale and faint as though shining from behind a veil.

The congregation headed down the back of the open hall, down a long length which led to the back of the cathedral. Here, once upon a time, the whole of Areglos's clergymen had their apartments, their places of study and of worship, now long abandoned and left to rot, even as the rest of Kirklyn, it seemed. For though the nearer chambers looked merely unoccupied, albeit untidy, further down the hall, the chambers began to shew signs of fungoid moss growing along the spaces between bricks, along the floors and seemingly transforming all the furniture and books into lush, green hills and fungoid flora. The sight brought to mind some visions Dashiell had seen after his communion with the Great One:

Perfect and bounteous lands, ripe for reaping and sowing to feed the once destitute lands of Kirklyn. Its people had grown so much faster than the resources available to them. Then, like a gift from the very heavens, the Great One came. For only a bit of its flesh, wondrous visions and knowledge were given—and by those visions, the Church of Areglos was able to provide for the people in such a way as no king or mayor ever had. But at what price? It was always assumed that Orianna had been too greedy of the visions—and who could blame her? Even the most mundane of them were like a rush of creative vision. Not once were the visions disappointing or mundane.

Dashiell had been brought into the fold of the Inner Circle early on, ere he began to question Mallory's intentions. Given his involvement—at least to the extent he was involved—Dashiell knew the history of the Great One better than most. Better than Bram or Mavis— better than dead, suffering Mad Mortimer and the Gluttonous Orianna. Indeed, this whole affair now rang uncomfortably similar to Stowshaw. It demanded answers as to how this had occurred again, and there was no doubt Mallory had them—though it was unlikely he could communicate such truths any longer.

It was amidst these thoughts that they at last reached the end of the hall, and came before an uncanny fusion of nature and science. An elevator of sorts—the first of its kind in Kirklyn or any known city in the world. Mallory himself had the vision from the Great One and under his instruction, brick by brick, the old staircase had been taken out and this stone platform was put in its place. Chains and a lever worked the thing. Magic it certainly was not, but a marvel to the whole of the clergymen for a long, long while, all the same.

Since the Inner Circle had withdrawn to the upper floor of the Cathedral, the elevator was kept above, and none had been seen descending or ascending it for months—save for the insane blasphemies which now guarded access to the Great One. Just as Dashiell and the others had expected, the stone platform sat at the bottom of the shaft, waiting for the hideous, worm-like creatures to return.

Down from the open shaft came a thick, pollen-choked air. It smelled of foetid fungus and rot. One or two of the priests choked on the initial inhale fungoid air, coughing a few deep, rough coughs, but the others—including Dashiell—seemed immune to the air, and even as he breathed it in, Dashiell felt his skull begin to writhe happily.

*What have we become?*

Like the air, the moss and fungus grew most thick here, coating the shaft, the doorway, even the floor. Amongst the living moss, there were other strange growths—these having purple or pinkish hue and being somewhat translucent, though having more in common to flesh than to vegetation. Indeed, the moss seemed alive—almost sentient—and Dashiell felt a cold chill steal down his spine, as though the very walls themselves were aware of the clergy's presence and were watching.

But it was now or never, and Dashiell swallowed hard before stepping onto the platform. The others slowly and somewhat reluctantly followed. Then young Deacon Julian, last of all, pulled down the lever and hopped onto the platform as it began its slow ascent into the blackness above.

# III

The elevator creaked upward whilst the eight clergymen stood silently, torches in hand, all spaced apart on the wide, circular, stone platform. The going was slow, enough for them all to notice how thick the darkness became, and how little light their torches and candles seemed to offer. Dashiell in particular still seemed quite certain the fungoid moss was watching them—though there was no presence of eyes that he could see. The others must have had some sense of this as well, even if they did not voice it aloud or even admit it to themselves, for Dashiell could sense the tension amongst them. By the fading light of their makeshift torches, Dashiell could see the faint glitter of perspiration on one or two foreheads. Only Deacon Julian seemed unfazed, though Dashiell knew better than to believe the youth did not have a single apprehension about the unknown above— the unknown which the youth looked directly up into with his cool eyes.

He was brave for certain, Dashiell mused. Perhaps he would have made a great Reaper had he chosen a different path in life. Dashiell smiled despite himself, and this Julian must have caught, thinking it unlike the older priest, for he looked down from the pitch dark above and toward Dashiell. Whatever Julian's expression in return, Dashiell did not see, for at that moment the faint, fading light of his torch sputtered out as though blown by a disembodied and non-existent breath, and so too did all the lights go out that the clergymen carried.

A few of them cried out, drowning out the monotonous clink of the chains pulling the platform up toward the darkness above.

"Silence!" hissed Dashiell, as a hand touched his shoulder.

Dashiell assumed it had been Julian, but he did not turn to look, for more important was the reason for the sudden interruption. Slowly a very faint light began to glow in the air, no brighter than a lightning bug, and like such a creature, the dull, faint light faded unevenly in and out. The light had no warmth to it, no wondrous orange-gold. It was a sickly green light, and it came from the spores which floated lightly about the air, thicker now than they had been at the base of the shaft. With them came the foetid stench of fungoid rot—so thick Dashiell felt he could almost chew on it. Yet, despite this, the taste of rot felt calming to him, as though it were a beloved childhood blanked and a bite of his favourite treat. He grew angry for the fact, silently cursing the wrath Mallory had brought down upon them.

The chain continued to clink along, and there was a hard clunk followed by uncontrollable coughing from one of the clergymen.

At least one of them, it appeared, did not have quite the same reaction to the fungoid air as Dashiell—or rather, lack of reaction. Dashiell watched coldly as the man bent over, choking, and coughing whilst the spores danced about the air. It was a strange thought that occurred to Dashiell just then: that it had been quite a while since he had seen Deacon Campbell take communion—longer than many of the others who were present.

Barely audible over the man's fit, Dashiell heard the clunk of the chain followed by a grinding sound. The platform began to jerk, wiggling in its narrow space. Dashiell turned and by the faint glow of the spores, he made out that the clergymen were all quite near the top of their ascent. He turned to make the others aware, and then he was thrown down to the hard stone platform as the elevator ground to a sharp and uneven halt.

The bones in Dashiell's knees and the palms of his hands ached—the skin over them stinging as though a fork had been repeatedly scraped along them. Somehow, he had avoided smashing his face into the stone platform. He opened his eyes. Despite his uninjured head, the room spun in an unfocused haze—or rather had spun and could no longer right itself, as though everything stuck at an odd angle, and he felt a force pulling him toward the corner where the stone platform met the wall.

He heard groans around him, and Deacon Campbell's incessant coughing continued. Dashiell began to push himself upright, but it all felt wrong, as if he had somehow managed to push the floor away from himself, rather than himself away from the floor. There were a few loud cries from the others, a scraping followed by a clunk. Dashiell fell back to the floor. The lights around him continued to fade in and out.

Dashiell attempted to push himself upright again, his shoulder feeling as though it weren't quite fitting properly in its place after the second fall, but he managed well enough. His shoulder cracked back into place. There was another groan as of a machine moving into action, impotently. The floor quaked, but Dashiell managed to gain his feet. Immediately, he lost them again and went stumbling toward the corner of the platform. He collided against something, but it was not the wall. He blinked. Something soft but firm. The lights were going in and out, but Dashiell was beginning to orient himself again. He saw the others rising to their feet as well, stumbling this way and that. Deacon Campbell, however, remained on the ground coughing. Dashiell turned and saw Deacon Julian was with him.

"Are you all right, Deacon?" said the youth.

Dashiell squeezed his wrist by way of affirmation.

The elevator had nearly reached the upper floor, but had come to a halt and was now leaning at a severe angle seemingly wedged within the shaft—one end but three feet from the upper floor. The floor felt unstable. As he looked about the platform, Dashiell could see the chains which helped to operate the mechanism were intact—but everywhere there was moss, so that there seemed almost more of it than masonry at this point.

"Moss must have gotten into the gears," said Julian.

"Hurry!" said Dashiell, as much in answer to Julian as to the others. "We'll need to climb out."

Though this last statement seemed a redundancy, as Deacon William and Crossley were already helping each other to reach the high end of the platform. But if Dashiell's words were not enough to move the others to action, a slight grinding of the platform was the fire of motivation they needed.

Despite the need for immediacy, it was a slow climb. Fortunately, Dashiell had Julian's aid, and by it he was able to keep his footing, fighting the sloped pull of gravity and the ache in his knees. Only twice did he almost fall, as Austin had done, sliding along the platform to near the lower corner where it was wedged against the wall. Within a minute, Julian was running back to the aid of Deacon Austin, whilst William and Crossley helped Dashiell and Deacon Uzziah up onto the upper floor. Julian himself came back with Austin, and helped himself up.

The group looked to each other, silently counting heads and identities, when they noticed the absence of two amongst their ranks. Then, for a while unheeded in the heat of it all, they again noticed the coughs of Deacon Campbell, and saw that he still lay on the tilted platform, as Deacon Asa struggled to get him to stand. Yet every time it seemed the attempt was going well, Deacon Campbell would again fall into a fit of coughing, sending him back to his knees. Upon the last one, Campbell wretched, and a black, discoloured phlegm spilled upon the ground.

*Just how long had it been since he had taken communion?* Dashiell wondered. The fate of the priesthood was not the same as the denizens of Kirklyn, as Orianna and Mortimer had sinfully tested in Stowshaw, when the Great One became angry with its protectors for their gluttony. *Then why did that look like the Rot?*

"Asa! Leave him!" Uzziah cried.

Then the platform groaned and sunk another half-foot. A loud metallic crack was heard as one of the chains broke and the platform ground against it. Campbell fell forward again. Deacon Asa kept his feet, but not his head.

"Help!" he screamed.

Another grinding and the sound of the broken chain coming loose and falling through the shaft. Julian went to run toward the helpless clergymen, but Dashiell held him. Another chain snapped. Asa screamed. Deacon Campbell, seeming completely unaware of the danger, continued to cough. The platform ground again, and the second chain came loose. Then all at once, the platform nearly righted itself, jerking itself to a momentary, horizontal halt. But such weight the two remaining chains could not bear. They snapped with a loud crack.

Deacon Asa looked directly at Dashiell, though he did not scream this time. Tears welled in his eyes and Dashiell could barely hear the sound of Asa's voice being caught in his throat, but along his spine, he could feel the cold, tingling terror that he knew Asa must have felt as he disappeared into the pitch black below.

# IV

Not one of the remaining clergymen spoke a word as they stared down into the black maw that had swallowed their two confederates. The dull echo of stone smashing against stone had long faded, and not another sound escaped the black, moss-choked throat.

At length Dashiell turned away, and the others followed his lead. An odd, inexplicable sense of calm stole over him. Perhaps it was the thrill of having escaped death mixed with the exhaustion of the harrowing moments which now lay behind them. Or perhaps it was something else. Numbness over the death of his two companions? Dashiell thought it unlikely, but there was a silver lining in the tragedy: that elevator was the only known entrance to the Upper Cathedral, and now those blasphemous, once-human worms would be unable to trouble them—or at least, it would slow them down. There was some comfort in that. They would have more time to reach the Great One. Dashiell sighed audibly.

The others still did not make a sound as they stepped out into the winding corridors of the Upper Cathedral. Not even their slippered feet made the least scraping noise against the stone, for there a mold most foul and choking had all but consumed the marbled masonry that had once stood in finely carved white and grey beauty—much changed since the last time Dashiell or any of the others had set foot above.

It had not been entirely unaffected by the growing fungus when last Dashiell had visited that upper floor— an early confirmation of Mallory's growing gluttony— but it was yet at the time much as the lower floor was now: with hints of moss and fungoid growth covering furniture and decorative objects and between the cracks and crevices of the brick work of the walls. Now the Upper Cathedral looked like a veritable forest of rot, with black, green, and brown fungus covering all in sight but for the slightest shoots of brick and masonry peeking out like the vine-choked boughs of dying trees.

Here also there grew bits of mushroom-like fungus, and in the thickest patches, the hairy texture of the moss was lengthened and waving in the breeze-less, still air like the tentacles of some ocean dwelling mutation. And among the fungus and tendrils were those same translucent growths, bubble-like and gelatinous—as though made from the same substance as a jellyfish. At those points in particular Dashiell seemed fixated, sensing a sentient awareness in them, as though the very walls were watching and calculating the clergymen's every movement. There was even the dull impression that the walls could read Dashiell's thoughts. He shook off that last unreasonable fear with a twitch of his shoulders.

The air felt moist, so much so that there was a sensation as if swimming in it, yet it felt cool and comforting. Like in the elevator shaft, there was still the same dull throbbing light from the floating spores, and now too the gelatinous growths had a light of their owe: some indescribable colour that might have been purple, or red, or green, or blue. All around them they heard a soothing dripping and the calming sound of ocean waves, though there was no visible water anywhere.

Despite the changed visage of the halls, their layout was not changed. All of them knew the location of the Bishop's chambers and of the small chapel the clergy used for their own worship in days long gone and which had been converted into the secret home of the Great One. They all as one stepped out and to the right, keeping their eyes open and their ears alert, despite the relative sense of safety they presently felt. They did not have far to go, however, ere that sense was broken.

After only a few short steps and rounding a corner on their right, the clergymen saw by the unstable light of the spores the crumpled form of something in their path, and though the light was too faint to discern the precise nature of the form, they all knew at once that it was not a heap of moss. As Dashiell drew closer, followed by the others, the body of a person came into view, covered in black rot and with its ripe, eyeless head torn open, its fluid-like nectar all but drained. What little remained of the corpse's brain fluid glistened in the throbbing spore light, and Julian moved forward and bent down over the body.

"There's a tinge of warmth," said the priest, as he held up fingertips coated with viscera. Dashiell heard one of the men behind him let out a low groan.

Dashiell wasted no time stepping over the corpse, careful not to slip on its leaking innards, as he led the men further into the halls and toward the chambers of Bishop Mallory and the inner chapel. They had barely moved forward a few feet when a second sight was brought into focus, and this one sent a chill even down Dashiell's otherwise hardened spine.

There upon the wall on their left hung a cocoon-like sack, strung up with wet membranous string, similar to the translucence sprouting about the mold. Dashiell could feel cold sweat beading on his neck as he stared at it. Just through the strings of the membranous sack, and by the fading in-and-out light of the spores, Dashiell saw a man's nose and two closed eye lids. The clergymen drew closer.

"Clay!" exclaimed Uzziah.

Though but hours since a few of that group brought him to the infirmary, already Deacon Clay was undergoing a strange metamorphosis: his body somewhat losing its form as bone twisted and dissolved, and his skin stretched in places, changing colour, and giving the slightest indication of forming strange, tentacle like appendages. Dashiell silently thanked the Great One that Clay's eyes were closed. Though Clay—

the man—did not shew any signs of life, these new, boneless appendages that grew from him wriggled impotently like some newborn squid reaching for its first sustenance. At his hip, Dashiell felt a wriggling sensation, as though his own body were answering some unconscious instinct. He wondered if the others too felt a similar sensation where the Great One had cursed them. *Such a fate was not fair to be brought upon us all in retaliation for Mallory's avarice. Kirklyn will not become another Stowshaw. We will fix this, and put things to rights.*

Whether Deacon Crossley felt the same tickling sensation as Dashiell is unknown, but the sight of Deacon Clay strung up, seemingly lifeless, in such a state, broke the man's mind, and he ran screaming into the dark, back in the direction from which they came. Deacon Austin attempted to physically restrain him, and Dashiell opened his mouth to yell after him, but the terror of the man was so great it caused them all to falter, and Dashiell's voice caught like a lump in his throat. The remaining five could do naught for a moment but stand there frozen dumb and listen to the man's screams dwindle into the otherwise silent dark.

Then, there was a choking final cry and silence fell.

The five remained still for a moment, listening for any hint of Crossley's fate. Had he attempted to climb down the shaft? Had he cast himself down it in a last mad attempt to escape horrors too great to bear? No sound of a thud, however dull, came down the silent halls, nor was there any sound of struggling. There was no sound at all, at first, but slowly, growing, another sound wriggled its way through the darkness. It was a faint sound and they could not quite place its nature. They strained their ears, wondering if the sudden terror of Deacon Crossley was not causing some delusions of their own when suddenly there came a new sound, this one clear and horrifically loud:

An otherworldly and inhuman screech.

# V

The blood of the clergymen ran cold as that screech echoed through the halls. Dashiell could feel his entire form, even his heart, freeze for a moment—all of his form except the uncanny, tickling movement in his hip. Not so much as a gasp escaped any of their lips, though a few members of the dwindling group's eyes began to sting from the salt of held back tears. That inhuman, impossible, blasphemous screech, coming from no creature of this world had been heard many times within the cathedral and amongst the streets of Kirklyn these past months. Though the poor, Rot-infected denizens seemed to have much reason to fear those sounds and the creatures who uttered them, those of the clergy who were not part of the Inner Circle did not believe they needed to be terrified of the worm-like things—*hadn't they known them once, after all? And would not Mallory's actions bring them closer still?* But the misguided assumption that there was nothing to fear from those insane larvae had been easier to delude themselves with before Dashiell and his men had come into the Upper Cathedral—a place which had been sealed off to them even before

Mallory had stopped sending messages to those below. Now, the five remaining deacons were actively and openly working against Bishop Mallory, and they no longer felt so certain of their assumptions.

A second screech rang out, hardly closer than the last, but this one seemed to have the effect of convincing the clergymen of the cold reality of their situation and inspire their limbs to movement. Though their muscles shook uncontrollably, the men fought to turn and race down the corridor. As a whole, they ran in the direction of the Inner Chapel and Mallory's private chambers. The soft, mossy floor helped dull the sound of their racing footsteps, though their hearts began to beat so rapidly and heavily, they feared the horrors behind could hear the thumps against their chests. Dashiell's hearing was keen, and even over the loud throbbing of his heart, he could hear the sinister slithering of slime covered worms moving along a sleek surface—a sickening, squishing sound—and with it came the twisting tickle in his hip. He stumbled and nearby Julian caught him and helped him to his feet. Then came another, otherworldly screech, and looking back, they saw by the dim, throbbing light, worm-like, tentacled forms.

Dashiell needed no further urging from Julian and by the sheer will for survival he righted himself and began to run. With him was Julian and Deacon Uzziah. Deacons Austin and William had gotten ahead and appeared to have no care whatever to assist their companions in escape.

None of them dared look back as the cold sounds of slithering and screeching continued to echo from behind. He heard Austin let out a scream and stumble forward. For his part, William paused a moment, staring dumbly at Deacon Austin sprawled forward upon the floor crying out for Deacon William's help. But once Dashiell and the others overtook them, the frozen William turned and ran. Deacon Austin let out a scream so terrifying it turned Dashiell's stomach to the point he thought he would sick all over the rotting floor. He silently thanked the Great One that Austin's voice was at last snuffed out by the sound of sucking and slurping. But Austin's regrettable distraction was not enough slow down the unnameable creatures. A few of the worms had stopped to feast, but Dashiell heard the sound of the majority continuing the pursuit—and those sounds came not only from behind them.

Racing past one of the halls which ran perpendicular to their path, Dashiell saw two of the horrors shambling down the corridor toward them. The things let out a wailing screech. A throbbing ran through Dashiell's entire form, emanating from the undulations in his hip. It nearly made him lose his balance again, and he caught himself against the wall. It was wet with moisture and squishing moss, but Dashiell was able to slide forward and back onto his feet proper, continuing beside his companions. Yet even as the throbbing passed, disorientation persisted, for so changed were the upper halls now, and in places the moss had grown so thick, that even Dashiell did not recognise where they were.

Nearly his entire life he had called the Grand Cathedral home, and for much of that time he had been amongst those given access to those upper halls. Until only a few months ago, when Mallory sealed off the Upper Cathedral, Dashiell had walked those halls, and yet now they seemed entirely unknown to him. The chambers and halls all looked the same, with their moss coverings and no distinguishing marks, and in some places the moss was thick enough to block a passage entirely. Worse still, the more they ran, the more confused the way became.

Twisting and turning they all of them ran through the foetid labyrinth, as the slitherings and screechings continued around them. Deacon Uzziah turned left. The others turned right. Dashiell could no longer hear the heavy breathing of William behind him.

With all his will for survival, Dashiell fought against the tickle in his hip which surged up every time the foul creatures screeched. His thighs throbbed, turning near-rubbery in their exhaustion even without the tickling to twist them. His breath came in gasps, and he could not quite get the air down into his lungs for the sharp pain which rose beneath the right side of his ribcage.

One corridor opened into another after another. A turn here. A mossy obstacle there. How long they ran on, Dashiell could not be certain, nor could he be certain that they had not merely run in circles. He no longer cared if they reached Bishop Mallory's chambers. He just wanted to be out of this maze.

He and Julian turned another corner and by chance they saw Deacon Uzziah racing toward them, though their blood ran cold to see by the spore-lights that out of the shadows three of the blasphemous things were close behind Uzziah. He smiled. The sight of friendly faces washed all the horrors away for just a moment. Evidently, he was unaware of the imminent danger, for when one of those creatures let out its gluttonous cry, Uzziah froze, staring at Dashiell in disbelief, as though somehow the clergyman could have saved his life. By sheer luck a hall crossed between them and Julian turned down it, and Dashiell followed him, but not before seeing those hideous tentacles close around Uzziah. One of the screeching worms lifted the deacon into the air as it forced its toothy tendrils down the man's throat and through his eyes. Dashiell was thankful Uzziah had not been able to scream as had Deacon Austin.

The slurping and crunching of bones echoed after them, slowly dying away only by their decreasing proximity. Dashiell felt he could hardly go on, but the tireless youthful, energy of Julian and the fear of the horrors behind motivated him well beyond the abilities of his age. *Perhaps*, Dashiell wondered, *it is a power of communion with the Great One or a side effect of the cursed life which writhes within me now.*

They had gone only a little further when Dashiell marked a change in the air. There was a humid chill to the atmosphere, as if the outside was coming in. The lighting was different and he noted also that he no longer heard the slithering pursuit of the worm-like creatures. It occurred to him then that perhaps they had come to the short outer bridge that led from upper floors of the cathedral at the front to those in the back: and there was the inner chapel and the chambers of Mallory himself.

Forgetting his fears, and spurred on by the excitement of this new realisation, Dashiell nearly overtook the youthful Julian. He saw the wide-open door before them and in it stood a twisted and bent figure.

Deacon William looked upon the approaching couple with wide eyes, leaning against the side of the portal to keep himself upright. His face was flushed red and his form looked soaked with perspiration. He breathed with great effort, and his body moved up and down with each breath as though he were trying to work up the energy to make a sound. His body trembled as though his last nerve were about to snap.

He began to raise a shaking finger to his lips, but too late as Julian—perhaps from excited relief or from that lack of perception so common to the young—called out William's name. Then William began to shake even more, and Dashiell could see his eyes redden and wet. At last, he began to speak—or at least attempted to—but all that came out were the mad babblings of a broken mind. As they neared him, they saw that the man's leg was twisted at an impossible angle, as though a hideous force had gripped and crushed it.

How William had managed to drag himself away from the clutches of those things and crawl his way to that door was a wonder. But even had William not seemingly lost the ability to speak of the ordeal, there would have been no time to ask questions. William's expression told them all they needed to know, even before the deafening screeches echoed from behind. Those sounds were so much closer than seemed possible given the silence which preceded the moment.

With so little strength remaining to them, Julian and Dashiell ran for the door. William merely let out a pitiful sob and fell to the floor, shaking uncontrollably as tears streamed down his face. It was as though the man were dead already, and the form of his body merely twitched in its final moments of blood-pulsing life.

Dashiell ran through the doorway with Julian at his side, though Dashiell gained the lead when Julian turned to help William to his feet, useless as was the gesture. Even his youthful speed could not match the horrific swiftness of those tentacles, nor could his strength overcome his own stress and exhaustion.

With a trembling gurgle, William was pulled into the air and all Julian came away with was the bloody stump of William's forearm as his still trembling, living form was forced upward toward the fanged maw of the blasphemous worm. Behind it, others of its kin came forward to share in the prize, and Julian ran, in his panic still holding onto William's disembodied arm. His youth was all the advantage he needed, for just as Dashiell was opening the door at the far end of the short bridge, Julian had nearly reached him—but so too had four of the worm-like horrors.

They let out an excited screech, and Dashiell stumbled over the threshold as the writhing tickle in his hip answered the cry. He turned to see Julian nearly upon the doorstep, and the four blasphemous creatures nearly upon the young deacon. With the last of his strength, Dashiell leaped up and grabbed the inward swinging door. He then threw himself against it even as Julian reached the doorway. The youthful priest crashed against the slamming barrier on the other side.

Dashiell kept his back to the door and slid down to

the floor, as Julian screamed and pounded against the door with those strong, youthful hands. Dashiell merely sat and listened as the life was taken from them to the crack of bones and the slurping of viscera, and as Julian's gurgling, mindless cries played a song for that hideous feast.

# VI

Dashiell woke to silence. He looked about the hazy dark trying to recall his recent ordeal. His heart froze when at last his mind recalled the horrified expression in Julian's eyes. Recollection came flooding back, nearly suffocating him. Dashiell did not wish to move. His plan had gone awry, and now he wished that all the world would disappear around him. He was no less good than Mallory. Let the Rot take it all—and it would, but only if he remained seated there on that floor.

Perhaps the illusion of him bearing the whole survival of mankind on his shoulders was the only ego-driven thought that inspired his body to move. Perhaps it was a desire to confront Mallory once the Great One had been safe. Perhaps it was merely some primordial instinct that his long years among the clergy had all but snuffed out and quelled. Men were not beasts, but whatever was occurring in Kirklyn now was certainly challenging that belief. It had been for a long time. Even Dashiell was uncertain if he could hold on to his humanity.

Whatever the reason for his movement, with a

shaky resolve he slowly rose to his feet, using the door at this back to steady himself. His muscles were stiff and ached, but other than the crack of his knees, and the pop of his hip, no other sound issued on either side of the door. Still, Dashiell waited. He wanted to scream, to make any sound or movement to help drown out the horrors that were spinning through his mind, but he dared not. He stood, holding his breath for fear it might drown out even the least sound of warning of danger.

Silence.

His heartbeat throbbed in his temples, and soon the silence became as unsettling as the screeches of the worm-like creatures who had brought this damned nightmare upon them. Yet still he waited. He shook with anticipation until his chest felt about to burst. He began almost to desire to open the door and run back from where he came. With growing paranoia, Dashiell began to wonder if Mallory had not remained behind as the others went out to hunt. Was he alone? Was Mallory waiting just beyond one of the doors leading off the chamber? Had Dashiell run directly into his trap?

He resisted the urge to flee and no sounds came from beyond the door or within the chamber or those rooms beyond. There were no sounds of the slithering of those insane creatures. At last Dashiell let out a slow, long, silent sigh.

With each intake of breath and exhalation, Dashiell allowed himself to feel just ever so slightly safer than by the breath before it. He moved his eyes feverishly as he looked about the chamber in which he now stood. To the left of him was the door of Bishop Mallory's office, to

the right the church head's bedroom—also Mallory's—
and in front of him stood the half-closed door of the
converted private chapel that had become the home of
the Great One following its rescue from Stowshaw.
Though Dashiell himself knew the small chapel and had
been to visit Bishop Mallory's office a handful of times,
even someone new to those rooms could have seen that
they were not in any sane condition.

Like the halls of the Upper Cathedral from where
Dashiell had come, the chamber here was made more of
moss and translucent polyps than of stone—perhaps
even more so than anywhere else in the cathedral or in
Kirklyn beyond. The entire floor was moss covered, and
great translucent growths grew amongst the mold along
the walls. Though these transparent carbuncles were
much larger and seemingly more aware than those in the
former chambers. Looking at them, Dashiell felt
exposed, as though some preying entity had found him
and there was no longer any use in hiding. Lichen hung
like tapestries from the ceiling, and all about grew
mushroom-like and other impossible fungi. Dashiell
could see that it sloped and gathered toward the door of
the private chapel before him. Cold sweat ran down his
spine and through the wisps of hair at his temples.

*What had Mallory done? How insatiable had Mallory's
gluttony become? Was it so great that he had fully consumed the
Great One? Was this punishment of sin irreversible?*

Dashiell had never been to Stowshaw, and neither
Mallory nor Oscar nor Mavis had shared the full details
of the incident even with the Inner Circle. Even so,
Dashiell knew much, and this was far worse than any

reports of what Orianna had caused to happen in the now abandoned village. The whole purpose of bringing the Great One to Kirklyn was to guard it and ensure none would abuse its visions in such a way as had Orianna. Yet even amongst the learned, it seemed, history did repeat itself. Or perhaps Mallory thought himself above it?

Though his breathing had calmed, Dashiell still found the silence unsettling. *Surely,* Dashiell thought, *if the bishop were here, he would have heard me enter. Or could he be here and yet so deep into his visions, he was deaf to all else?* Dashiell knew how intoxicating and all-consuming those visions could be when one was in the midst of them. At that thought, he felt the writhing tickle in his hip.

He moved away from the door and took a moment to heap against the door whatever pieces of furniture and objects the Rot had not utterly consumed. Silence or not, he did not know if those things would return, nor if they were capable of working a door with those writhing appendages. And if Mallory were there, waiting for his insane-kin to return, there was no returning by that way now. It was up to Dashiell, alone and unaided, to save the Great One. If and once that could be accomplished, Dashiell would wait for the visions of his god to tell him what was next to be done. He would beg Its forgiveness on behalf of the people of Kirklyn. It was not their fault that Mallory had chosen to repeat the sins of Orianna and turn a blind eye to the wrathful warning the Great One brought down upon Stowshaw.

It was slow work to cover the door sufficiently enough that Dashiell could feel reasonably secure in his barrier. He was exhausted still, even after sleep had taken him for however long, and he moved as softly as he could. All the while, Dashiell heard no screeches from the other side of the door, nor any sound or movement came from this side of it—only the seeming sentience of the silent mold watching him at his task.

Once done, Dashiell took up one half-rotten piece of wood, likely a leg from a table, which had a pointed end. He would not be taken unarmed. With trembling knees, Dashiell turned his attention first to Mallory's bedchambers.

Inside Mallory's private chamber there was no sign that the bishop or anyone else had lived there in quite some time. Nearly everything was rotted away but for a curious heap on the moss-grown floor, half sucked into the rot.

Dashiell drew closer and bent down to see that it was the robes of a clergyman—specifically those bestowed upon a bishop. As Dashiell lifted it, his blood ran cold, and he began to shake uncontrollably. Strands of hair and what could only be described as melted flesh fell away with the membranous goo which Dashiell felt so reminded him of the state in which they found Deacon Clay.

Almost in a spasm, Dashiell stood up, but fell again and wretched his sick upon the rotting floor. His mind reeled with hideous thoughts, as the tickling increased in his hip and felt as though it were writhing through his stomach. It was not the confirmations of what he already knew to be true, but rather contact with what horrors still awaited him, if he could not make penance for

Mallory's sins.

Dashiell grabbed hold of the mold firmly, trying by physical touch of the real and present to keep the horrors from his mind which now threatened to break it. But the harder he squeezed, the more the tickling became an unbearable pain, until he wretched again, and stumbling toward the rotting wall, he rose, half consciously.

At least Mallory was not at home, so Dashiell could only assume, and the door was well blocked. He had some time, and the Great One awaited him—that is if It had not been consumed by Mallory completely. Then there would be no stopping this, no forgiveness to receive.

Dashiell began to shake again. His stomach turned. He wondered if Mallory, like so many of the clergy, did not keep a gun within a drawer somewhere—and hoped that the thing was not clogged with moss. A better end, he thought, than to endure the same twisted eclosion the Inner Circle had completed. Yet it was not his fear, or his thoughts of a more acceptable death that drove him forward in the end, but rather an immense curiosity.

Dashiell stooped to pick up the pointed, rot-eaten wooden leg again, though now he imagined little use in it. He crossed the main chamber to the door opposite Mallory's bedroom: the door to the bishop's private office.

# VII

The Rot had seeped into nearly everything. Books and papers were black with mold, and the furniture seemed to melt with moisture. Yet in the center of the room stood Mallory's desk, still mostly intact, and there upon it was a book of notably less deterioration than the others, a last bastion of humanity against the encroaching Rot.

Carefully, Dashiell picked his way through the room toward the desk. Like the translucent "eyes" of the mold, Dashiell felt a strange sense of fleshiness in the substance when looking at the floor, and he was afraid to tread too roughly upon it lest it become—*angry? No, that was impossible.* Yet somehow in that moment, the floor being alive seemed saner an idea than the reality of what Mallory and his followers had become.

With enough care, Dashiell was able to reach the desk. He lifted the book up and turned it over in his hand. It was a plain, leather-bound thing, with a strap to tie it shut. Contrary to the book's relatively clean aspect when seen from a distance and by comparison to the condition of the room, beneath its relatively unmarred cover, the book was heavily covered in mold.

With hardly a brush of his hand, the strap crumbled and fell away like dough, and when he opened it, Dashiell could see that little remained untouched by the consuming Rot. The binding snapped and half the book fell to the floor with a splat, it's pages heavy and creating a solid mush of paper. To the other half Dashiell held firm, but he was unable to make much of the writing at first. So rotted and discoloured were the pages he turned over, that he nearly abandoned it as useless to him. But then Dashiell turned upon a page with a date from two months past, written in Mallory's loose, looping hand. His journal—just as Dashiell had hoped.

The Rot made the reading difficult, as did the faint, swelling and dying light of the floating spores. Dashiell considered momentarily to look for a candle, but the moisture made him think twice about his ability to light anything—more so the seeming life of the room made him wary of any appearance of danger he might unwittingly present.

Leafing through the pages of the journal as best he could, many of the familiar names started to come into focus: Orianna and Mortimer, Mavis and Bram, Dayton, Stowshaw, and Kirklyn. Though unclear, Dashiell had the sense that Mallory was attempting to make some record of events, going back to the finding of the Great One, but this tale was often interrupted with small notes about the daily happenings in Kirklyn, Church initiatives, and even the building of the elevator to the Upper Cathedral. The Reapers too came into it:

> *Four more taken by the Rot today. Oscar sent Mavis with a small band of Church Reapers to the site. Three slain. One brought back to the infirmary...*

It was there, in the infirmary, that the Church of Areglos had hoped to heal those sick with Rot, but no results came of their experimentation. And once the other two Reaper lodges had been established, orderly acquisition of the sick became more difficult. Many were slain, as it was only the Church Reapers who were tasked with bringing the ailing to the Church. A horrible place the infirmary became too. A madhouse of swelling, lunatic creatures, strapped to beds. Over time, either the heads burst or by some unknown means, an infected might disappear from one day to the next. It was not until more lately that Dashiell suspected the fate of those once-people at the hands of Mallory and his followers.

But Dashiell shook off the nightmares of the past again, and continued to read on:

> *It was not I. I know it. I am certain I have been so careful. So, so very careful. Then who? Who? Or did something somehow escape the massacre at Stowshaw? But then why so many years later?*

As he read on, and even without the mold to fight with, it seemed that often enough, and with increasing frequency throughout the book, Mallory's hand appeared to be gripped with sudden spasm like fits, making the writing entirely illegible for a line or so. Worse still, these spasms often caused a seeming break in thought that was never returned to as whole threads were left unfinished mid-sentence.

*The punishment for his gluttony. That was when it began to take him. He must have known then he would not be immune.*

After one particular spasm, Mallory wrote what seemed to be an apology, and then commented on the writhing tickling in his arm. Dashiell thought of his hip and his blood ran cold.

> *The spasms continue with increased frequency, now. I have seen the concern in the eyes of others, at times, yet they will not confide in me. No doubt each man is afraid that he might be accused as the one who has brought this punishment down upon us. Yet I have heard no anger from the Great One when partaking of Communion. Indeed, the Great One still offers welcome visions of hope and prosperity for Kirklyn. Never once has it spoken to me with disappointment or condemnation.*

Dashiell had a difficult time believing that Mallory did not know the Great One was enraged with him. *Was he lying to himself? Madmen always convince themselves of their own fantasies.* Dashiell continued to read on:

> *What can be the source of this, then? Why has the Great One become angry?*

*So, he did know.*

> *Are the visions even a true interpretation of its communication with us? Are our small, human minds great enough to understand Its true purpose? I must believe the answers will be revealed in time. I must put my faith in the Glorious Great One.*

The writing of that particular passage ended there, but many passages seemed to follow the same thread: self-pity, self-denial, and a curious lack of self-reflection from a man otherwise so pious and intelligent. Compelled by a strange masochism, Dashiell continued to feverishly flip through the wet, soggy pages, trying to find some information that was more revealing. Mallory had long stopped his writings about the history of it all, and began to write more and more about his visions. The word "ascension" featured in the writings often. However, as Mallory wrote, the visions seemed to take on an increasing sense of dread.

> *Oh please, spare the poor children of Kirklyn. Let not my gluttony, unseen for the weakness of my humanity, bring punishment to all those innocents in its wake. Spare them and take me. I...*

But the writing cut off as it had in so many places, and for a page or two, either the writing was illegible or the book was too caked in Rot to make out much else but words "ascension" and "price of Communion". A few pages stuck together. Two had great gaping holes in them. Slowly the Rot cleared just enough again, and then Dashiell read, amongst a sea of unreadable lines:

> *...the Great One...name...we...and it was decided that to cut ourselves off and...from the rest of the Church...from the rest of Kirklyn. Our dear Church Reapers, they don't even know...must.. .away...*

More Rot and insane scribbling. Bram's name came up twice and Stowshaw, and then:

> *...Oscar is angry...so tired...who can blame...*

Followed again by Rot and some words written in a hand that was battling with itself too much to render any legible runes upon the page.

> *...mind feels open...half...One...thoughts not entirely my own...how long humanity will last.. .sentience...a connexion with...by the dear god we have abandoned...a devil...*

And then again, an insane spasm of writing, followed however nearly by a final passage wherein some of the words were completely illegible, no doubt because the hand which wrote them was no longer in full possession of the dexterous skill of working its pen:

> *...in Stowshaw...a fool...the Communion...we cannot harm it...it grows...the more we eat...*(and here a long set of scribbling followed before finally the hand righted itself long enough to barely scratch out): *...curse my blindness...Dayton was right!*

"Blasphemy!" Dashiell cried out and threw down the book. It sunk into the desk with a squish.

So, that was the way of it then. Whereas Fat Orianna had been unable to contain herself, Mallory had gone mad and thought to kill the Great One, just as the Visionless Traitor, Dayton, had so many years ago. And so, the Rot came to Kirklyn, not from the sin of gluttony, but rather a blasphemy against the Great One itself. But, the thought suddenly occurred to Dashiell, *is the Great One safe? Surely if It was, the nightmare would end!*

# VIII

As before, the main chamber which opened onto the bridge and three smaller rooms was silent and nothing moved save for the barely discernible undulations of the sentient growths of mold. Dashiell looked to the door that opened upon the bridge, heaped with broken furniture and unidentifiable wooden pieces. His rage had turned into panic—panic for the safety of his god— though an uneasy feeling turned in his stomach, and he could feel the tickling increase again, swelling in his hip, even as the spores in the air seemed to glow and fade brighter than before. Was it his imagination? Dashiell attempted to calm his breath, but sweat dripped from his temples and down his cheeks, and his hands began to tremble. He abandoned the pointed piece of rotten wood he had formerly hoped to use as a weapon. He would not need it in his audience with the Great One.

Dashiell felt himself growing dizzy, and the swelling tickle in his hip seemed to reach up into his ribs. He fell forward, cursing what Mallory had done to him. *If I could just make the chapel and speak with the Great One, all could be undone. Except for Mallory and his fold. Let them rot.* Dashiell could send the last of the Reapers to hunt them, ere retiring the title for good and all. Kirklyn would be saved, and never again would their just god send this plague against them.

The tickling twist in his hip did not decrease, but Dashiell could not allow himself to succumb to it so close now that he was to the Great One. Like a man whose legs have numbed with pins and needles, Dashiell had much difficulty rising to his feet, and he used the wall for balance. He pushed forward, slowly making his way to the door of the inner chapel, home to the Great One. Twice he stumbled into the wall. Once he fell altogether. He thanked the soft cushion of the horrible moss to keep his bones from bruising.

As he reached the door, Dashiell's mind buzzed with horrors half visualised as he twitched and tingled, his body surging with a strange pain. He squinted his eyes, trying to keep the thoughts away, trying to keep himself from going mad—trying to hold onto his humanity until the last. He made an effort to focus on the idea that once he stood before the Great One, his god would give him a vision that would help him to understand and offer the forgiveness he so desperately was attempting to gain for all of Kirklyn.

Slowly but methodically, he climbed a short hill of moss and came through the half-open doorway of the inner chapel. There within, Dashiell looked upon the cushioned bed of the Great One. It was propped up upon what had been an altar to their old god, the impotent one they had turned away from, for the glorious inspiration offered by the Great One. Such a strange little creature, Dashiell thought in that moment. How small and vulnerable It was for something so great and omnipotent. Indeed, it could not be left alone like this. Someone had to protect it, and protect it Dashiell would.

Dashiell heard a little titter coming from the bed, and he vaguely saw by the dull light the twitching of the Great One's limbs. He sighed, relieved. *So, Mallory had not been able to carry out his insane threat afterall.* He walked forward.

The little thing danced in Its crib before him, and Its deep eyes were open. Dashiell thought it strange, however, that the Great One seemed to have grown since he last looked upon it, rather than grow smaller, as he had expected given Mallory had been taking Communion with unchecked relish.

It called out to him, as It so often did, and Dashiell began to tear up for the beauty of Its voice, so long had it been since he had heard it. It was a joy to him. He knew the meaning of Its sounds, though It spoke no language known to Man: *take of my flesh.*

Then Dashiell began to weep and fell to his knees, clasping his hands together. It had been so long since he had taken Communion and heard the voice of the Great One, and his awe at his god's simple request made him weak with exultation. As though unconnected to himself, Dashiell heard his own voice speaking words of forgiveness and humility, but the Great One did not answer directly. Instead, It repeated Its request, and Dashiell took that to be the Great One's answer.

So, Dashiell, the tickle in his hip unrelenting, obeyed the wishes of his god and slowly rose to his feet. Soon the tickling would subside. Soon the Rot would wash away. Dashiell reached off to one side of the crib where a small, sharp knife was kept for the taking of Communion.

Dashiell passed the knife through the flesh of the Great One as through a tender morsel. The Great One twitched as though It giggled with elated welcome. Then

Dashiell put the sweet flesh upon his tongue and let it sit a moment as the visions began to wash over him like the waves of the sea at high tide. He could hear them now in all their glory. The wondrous gift of the Great One.

Tears continued to fall from his eyes, but soon his tears were no longer of joy. Dashiell grit his teeth, and his eyebrows furrowed. His entire body began to twitch and twist. The voice of the Great One. It had changed.

In a flash a vision—greater and more horrible than ever before—came to Dashiell, and all of the Eldritch Knowledge of the Great One was bare to him. He wanted to laugh, to cry, but he felt so distinctly that those faculties were already lost, melted away like flesh in a fire. The writhing in his hip began to swell through his entire body and with such intensity that he felt boneless, an invertebrate swelling of flesh, dancing in a moonlit meadow.

So intense was his rapture that the man who had been Dashiell both laughed and cried out in joy and terror. His mind broke utterly, as did his body. He was forgiven. Mallory was not his enemy, and the Great One welcomed Dashiell into itself.

But on the floor of the inner chapel, just before the crib of the Great One, a crumpled heap of clergyman's clothes lay, and lined in it was bits of gelatinous viscera and wisps of hair.

# Farren

# I

The sky flashed white as lightning cut through grey-black clouds. Not two seconds passed ere the rumbling boom of thunder followed. It had not been raining when they five had set out from Kirklyn. Not even the faintest hint of storm cloud had been in the sky then.

*Did the rain spread the Rot more quickly?* wondered Farren, as he looked up into the sky. All that tainted black mold, drinking up the moisture, riding the waves of trickling rain along the roofs and streets, onto the soles of people's shoes, into their homes. *Or was it the other way around? Did the rain wash it away, clean the streets as it would a blood-soaked battlefield? Did it stay the spread? Did it have no effect at all?*

So little about the Rot was known, even more than a year under its shadow, and despite all the efforts of the Church and the Reapers. Even after Stowshaw. *What even was the purpose of going? An immolated monument of failure. Nothing there but ashen rot. Or—would the rain rejuvenate whatever had dried up there?*

Another bolt of lightning cut across the sky, and

Farren counted just a half-second more than had been between the previous bolt and the following thunder.

The Old Reaper turned away from the sky, his grey beard moist from the rain despite the fair covering the dilapidated shed offered to him and his companions. *All of them were far too green—much like Evelyn. Bram's niece or not, who was she to assume the leadership of the last of them?* They didn't have the discipline or fortitude of the Old Reapers—those former Shields of the Church—nor did they experience the horrors that had come as a side effect of the serum they were given by the Church of Areglos.

Farren felt he could use some of it right about now. His bones ached, but not from age. Farren was robust for a man of fifty-some years and stronger than two of his youthful companions together. No, it was a stiffening of the joints that came from withdrawals of a lack of serum. *Bram's Curse* the Old Reapers called it, for Bram had been the first to halt the imbibing of Communion and the first to succumb to it. Farren had not been there at his friend's end, but he was told it was not a pleasant death, nor had it been for any of the Old Reapers whom Bram's Curse took.

Still, half-petrified or not, what he would not have done to have a few of the Old Reapers with him.

"This rain," said a thin youth who sat in the middle of the shed. He had only a small stubble of hair on his lip, and cut an awkward figure with a long jacket that was a bit too thick for him around the shoulders. Had not Farren known any better, the man could be mistaken for a tween of only sixteen or seventeen. The young man crossed his arms in front of him, rubbing them below his shoulders with the opposite hands. "Couldn't we light a fire?"

"No," said one of the others, a young man with longish hair, possibly having more experience than at least two of the others. Like Farren, he too had been looking up at the sky. "We're too close to Stowshaw now. Who knows what lurks out this way? Just don't sit under any holes in the roof, Kellen. You'll stay dry if not warm."

The hunched over Kellen in the slightly over-sized coat barely had a moment to nod in agreement when up walked a thick man, all bald with only a point of hair under his bottom lip. He smiled sardonically at Kellen as he held out his own coat toward the young man seated on the ground. He wore a tight, sleeveless shirt underneath, exposing massive, knotted muscles—much the opposite of Kellen, at least in looks. Farren knew his kind all too well, no less of a frightened, inexperienced boy than the companion he mocked, only somehow, he thought merely looking the part of a fighter would make him one. The Old Reaper couldn't decide whom he had less respect for.

"Don't mock him, Everett. It'll do no good to be at odds with one another on the road ahead. Church, Brave, and Bram's Cleansing Reapers—we're all one lodge now. There's no Church to guide us—none to rebel against."

Farren noted Robert did not use the derogatory "Cabbage," though none were in their unit. Then again, one could easily mistake Everett for being a member of that latest of Reaper groups. They had not had any of the Old Reapers to train them and paid dearly for it in the end. Only one remained, and Evelyn took him with her group. *What had his name been?*

Everett rolled his eyes and turned toward the man with the longish hair. "You're no fun, Robert," he said and then walked back to the pile of wood he had been using as a makeshift bench.

At least Robert had some sense.

Then there was the last of them, the fifth of the group. Robert seemed capable enough, though no one could say how a man might fare in battle until it came down to it, trained or not. Kellen and Everett were likely to be equally shite. But Jacoby. Something about Jacoby was hard to read. He always seemed calm—almost too calm for one who did not have the experience of Farren. Farren wondered why that would be.

Farren looked up at Jacoby, his shortish hair falling over his forehead as he scraped a whetstone along the blade of his sword. Farren could swear the man's eyes had just shifted, as though he had been staring at Farren until just before the old man looked up at him.

"We'll move on as soon as it lets up," said Robert. "Though I don't suppose that'll be before the sun rises."

The sun. Farren looked up toward the angry sky. A chill ran through him, aggravating the twisting grinding of his joints. The days in Kirklyn were much the same: all fog and cloud. The Old Reaper wondered if he would ever see the sun again? Not if Bram's Curse took him before his time, and if this all had begun with the incident in Stowshaw, the abandoned hamlet would look no less grim than the city of Kirklyn.

Farren wondered then if Stowshaw truly would

have the answers they sought, and if so, would there be a cure? Was it possible even to reverse whatever this ailment was? Stowshaw was his last hope, and it was the only reason he had agreed to join this company and leave Kirklyn, else he would have preferred to die fighting the horrors in the city ere the Curse took him, one of the very last of the Old Reapers. He and Mavis and…

"Porter and Vernon," came Robert's voice, almost in answer to Farren's thoughts. Word was the Church had called them in again over two months ago, but there was no word from the Twins. It was the last order from Areglos—many assumed at the time it was a changing of the guards on the road to Stowshaw. It was not long after that Mavis went away, too, but rumor was it was Oscar who sent the message. It was Oscar who had trained all the Old Reapers.

"Right. The Twins. Do you suppose they still live, or do you think the…" at this Kellen's voice trailed off, and he gave Farren a quick glance. Farren could not help but smile despite himself. "Do you think they've withered away?"

"We won't know until we reach Stowshaw, or near enough," answered Robert. "But Jacoby was amongst those that returned from the first trip. And those who reported back said the Twins still lived then."

Kellen looked at Jacoby with a furrowed brow.

"I suppose," said Jacoby, not looking up from sharpening his sword, "in a month's time Bram's Curse could have taken them by now. It is a slow-moving disease." And though it was not more than half a beat, this time Jacoby did look up, and he looked directly at

Farren. Their eyes met, and neither man flinched. "Slower even than the Rot.

"But I can tell you, when I saw the Twins from a distance, they were a misshapen mess, and wandering in aimless circles. We'd do better to hope the Curse has progressed enough that they no longer recall their duty and have wandered off elsewhere to die."

Kellen seemed almost to go stiff with fear, but he was pulled out of whatever racing thoughts were torturing him when Robert rose to his feet and placed a gentle, calming hand on Kellen's shoulder before walking off to a corner of the shed. He laid down and placed his hat over his face.

Farren remembered the Twins. They were younger even than him, hardly more than boys when they joined the ranks of the original Church Reapers, when the serum was still given out freely, even outside of Communion. Farren recalled that Mavis often noted the new serum was less potent than what had been given to the Shields. As for the Twins, Farren never had the chance to learn much about them. They were not very long on the job when they were sent to guard the road to Stowshaw. Most amongst the Church Reapers felt it was that the Church didn't think the Twins very capable of Reaping, but guards were needed there—and guards capable enough, at that.

There was word that people out of Kirklyn were beginning to grow a bit too curious about the Rot's outbreak in Stowshaw, even before it came to Kirklyn. Bram certainly had helped to stoke that fire. The Church of Areglos wanted to ensure no one reached the nearby province. Their official position was that they did not want the old strain to be brought back to Kirklyn. But Bram spoke of another rumour—or at least a theory—and that had gained some hold over the Reapers' imagination for a time. Either way, the Twins' curious duty was an early warning that they had all failed to heed.

Farren shook his head. The rain was still coming down, but not quite as hard. He saw that Everett, like Robert, was already down and dreaming. Kellen simply curled up in the middle of the shed right where he had been seated. Jacoby sheathed his sword and placed it in a corner of the soggy room before bedding down as well.

Farren rolled down onto the ground and shifted about trying to find a comfortable position to sleep in. He had never had trouble sleeping just about anywhere through his long career as a Reaper, but that was before the Curse.

After a time, he found a good spot, and sighed with relief as the tension let out of his muscles. Through the darkness of his eyelids, he marked a flash of lightning, but however long it was ere the sound of thunder followed, Farren was asleep before he could hear it.

# II

Lightning flashed across the sky above the cathedral in Kirklyn, and Farren saw by its light that the place was much changed: its bricks looked wet and almost scale-like and its windows suggested a multitude of black, hollow eyes in the face of some nameless horror. It had no mouth to speak of, the main door acting as an outlet for mossy vines and roots which reached out tentacle like all through the streets of Kirklyn. Similar appendages, somewhat arm or wing-like, reached out from the sides and from higher up on the cathedral. The structure was covered in hair-like moss and lichen, and had not Farren known the structure so well, he might have not recognised it for the Grand Cathedral of Areglos.

Another bolt split the darkness, lighting up undulating red clouds, moving like waves in an ocean of blood as cries and screeches sounded from distant, unseen throats. Below this sat a blasphemous creature, crawled up from some Hellish Pit.

Farren's skin crawled with cold sweat—a feeling he was none too used—but such was his shock at the realisation of where he stood. He looked about him, trying to calm his breath, but the screams and otherworldly sounds assailed his senses. He grew dizzy. Wild-eyed. Not a single other structure of Kirklyn stood, all now fallen away to the fungoid Rot that he recalled had long begun to spread over the city. He wanted to scream. He saw the tentacle-like appendages reaching out, far beyond his range of sight, fading away into the foetid blood-fog. Stiff yet quaking, Farren turned back to face the creature of chaos. Was it Bram's Curse that made it so hard for him to move? Did it dull his senses? He wanted to cry. He was so small and so fragile, naked, but for his beard which would be no protection against the veiling threat of the nameless horror before him.

The blasphemous thing did not to notice Farren, but instead seemed to be searching. Its tentacles writhed with curious excitement, but then those cold, malicious eyes rested upon Farren, and he felt his bones begin to snap. But he did not fall, because even as the bones in his body popped, bruising his skin, his legs turned to ashen stone and petrified wood. He twitched and choked on a rotting bile that came up from the pit of his stomach, black moss spilling from his lips. The blasphemy leaned toward him, its eyes blinking with sharp fixation. Into those eyes, into those hollow windows which opened on the thing's core, Farren saw.

His eyes filled up with black blood, even as the petrification stole up his entire form. Then with one more flash of lightning, Farren at last let out a cry of babbling lunacy which mixed with the hellish sounds around him. His brain melted from his skull as his eyes burst into cloud of red and scattered into the bloodied sky.

# III

Not a sound of thunder or flash of lightning greeted Farren as his eyes shot open, but there was a chill in the air. His face pinched against the stiff pain of his initial stirrings. He had certainly experienced rougher sleeps, though his nightmares were worsening over time. He slowly twisted onto his side and looked up at the sky. All fog and cloud, but no rain—and no sun either. He frowned.

With a grunt he raised himself up to sit upon the ground, but he felt his bones grind painfully against each other, fighting him to the last against rising onto his feet. Farren wondered again if it was his age and the chill air cutting through well-worn, creaking joints? Or was it the Curse which worked its slow death upon him? Was that too the source of the nightmares?

He reached for the glove on his left hand and pulled it carefully from his fingers, gritting his teeth as he did. He had taken to wearing them even whilst he slept of late. Farren looked down at his twisted, misshapen fingers. Their form was like five tentacles starting from a head on the end of his wrist. Again, the thought came to him: *did Stowshaw also hold a cure?*

Farren could not recall where he had even come up with such an idea. Perhaps it was something he overheard. Perhaps a half-remembered rumour. Perhaps something Bram had suggested to him. It was difficult to remember things precisely. His mind would become as fogged as the sky—another side effect of the Curse? And yet, his dreams were so visceral and real.

The more pragmatic side of him attempted to move the twisted fingers, trying to get a sense of their usefulness or lack thereof. He quickly decided he would wield his mace with his right hand. He could not be certain his shield would be much use, anyway. As these thoughts worked through his mind, a cold, freezing sweat came over him as Jacoby stepped just into his field of vision. Farren hurriedly pulled his glove back on, though his face shewed none of his panic. He looked directly into the young man's eyes, remarking silently to himself how confident they seemed for one so relatively new to this. Even Robert's levelheaded leadership did not seem so sound. It was a look Farren recognised in those who had experience—more alike to Evelyn and the crew she took, but theirs was a very different mission and more likely to end in battle.

"We're headed out," said Jacoby, without dropping his gaze. Slowly and stiffly, Farren rose to his feet, using the wall for assistance and ignoring the hand Jacoby offered to him. He caught the mocking grin of Everett as he eyed the Old Reaper from across the shed. Farren grit his teeth, and his jaw tightened, but that was the extent of his expressed embarrassment. He might be older, but he was far more useful than they—only they did not suffer from the Curse.

Jacoby silently turned away and like Farren, joined the others in making ready to move on.

Kellen and Robert stood fully prepared. Kellen wore his long coat and a wide-brimmed hat, both worn and patched. He tied a scarf around his mouth. Gloves and boots he wore—as did every man of their unit. Above these, Kellen wore plates of metal armour on his shins and forearms. His belt held a short axe and a long knife. Farren thought him a poor example of a Reaper, but Miles had insisted the lad had his uses—and Miles, though insane, was no fool. Robert wore taller boots and longer gloves of a thick leather, but his only armour was a full plate arm piece worn on the left. His vest too was of a thick leather, sleeveless, but with metal clasps evenly spaced down the front. He wore a tricorn hat with a white feather, and he wrapped, almost mummy-like, a leather strap about his mouth and nose. Two shotels hung at either side of his waist.

Jacoby was retrieving his sword and pulling up the lapels of his coat, which ran only down to just above his knees. The lapels could be buttoned above, creating a mask of sorts, and above he wore a top hat. His shins, like Kellen's, were covered in plate armour, and he wore a coat of chainmail, unseen beneath his overcoat. Something else too he wore, something around his neck, though Farren was having trouble focusing his eyes on it. The effort it seemed was making him dizzy—no doubt another side effect of the Curse.

Farren walked up to the others, pulling his hood up atop his thinning hair. The hood was attached directly to the collar of his brigandine. A thick leather strap covered his nose and mouth, and he smelt the familiar wash of frankincense run through his sinuses. Otherwise, he wore thick boots and gloves, his shield strapped to his left arm. He held his mace in his right hand. The shield was an odd choice for a Reaper, but in the hands of Farren it was as much a weapon as his mace. Perhaps in the hands of someone like Kellen it would have engendered passivity, but not so for the Old Reaper. Even Everett knew well enough not to attempt to mock him for it. Though it seemed Everett was focused on prodding Robert now more than he.

"Masks on, Everett," said Robert, and otherwise Everett looked prepared for the journey. He wore chainmail leggings and short boots over this, a thick piece of plate around the bottom of his torso, but his arms and chest were exposed, showing off his massive, knotted muscles. He rested his slightly curved, long club over one shoulder. Tilting his head to one side, Everett boldly smiled at Robert. "Masks on. We're nearing Stowshaw."

"I can't breathe with it on," said Everett dishonestly. Reapers trained with their masks on, acclimating to the lower oxygen intake and strengthening their stamina. "Besides, Kirklyn is long behind us. No need for it."

"You don't have a choice," returned Robert.

"All men have choices."

"Indeed," said Robert, his eyes narrowing, the frustration in his voice evident only by its measured pace. "But you were put under my command. So, you have the choice of your mask or returning to Kirklyn on your own—a failure and a coward."

There was a twitch in Everett's eyelid. Farren tightened his grip on his mace, as he saw Everett's jaw tighten and his cheeks flush an ever so imperceptible red hue. How Farren would love a chance to show the boy what real strength was. But whatever thought was moving about in Everett's head, it quickly passed. His eyelids fluttered a few times, and he spit on the ground, not directly at but not exactly away from Robert's feet. He picked a modified sallet out of his bag. It had a larger opening for the eyes to look through, and the front face-guard was lowered well over the mouth and chin, the metal band grated in such a fashion as to give it the shape of teeth.

This seemed to satisfy Robert, and Farren loosened his grip on his weapon. Then they all of them shouldered their packs for the journey and left the small shack behind them.

# IV

Just outside the walls of Kirklyn, the Rot seemed to clear up, leaving the trees and grass to grow as they once had: lush and colourful. They were all old enough to remember the bountiful land which grew up around Kirklyn and reaching out into the nearer hamlets, except toward Stowshaw where none were permitted to go, but Farren was older still. Though he never saw the withered lands as they had been ere the great bounteous harvests that suddenly turned Kirklyn's fortunes around, he was old enough to have heard the stories of the famine and disease that had struck the city before it had grown so grand—long before the coming of the Rot.

As they drew nearer to Stowshaw, Farren wondered if the land they now looked upon was nearer to what it had been all that time ago in Kirklyn and the surrounding hamlets. The landscape looked as though it had returned to the blight which had consumed it in time out of memory. It was no longer tended to by its people as they suffered under the growing Rot. *Or was this blight from the Rot itself? The disease seemed to infect everything it touched. Had the Rot then always been there, and somehow the Church's prayers had kept it at bay long enough for Kirklyn to flourish for a time? But that couldn't be, else how would any of this land have been settled in the first place?*

Indeed, it seemed like the Rot of Kirklyn and the Old Rot of abandoned Stowshaw were as two arms reaching out to one another. Though the more Farren saw of the metamorphosed landscape, the more he likened it to two riverbeds, one flowing, the other dried up and that once the two had met again, the dried up river—Stowshaw—would flow wildly again with the Rot which had once claimed it.

Though here, as in Kirklyn, the sky was ever sunless and grey, there was a dryness nearer Stowshaw which contradicted Kirklyn's moisture. Where the stones of the city seemed almost consumed by the black, foetid, mossy Rot, here not the least thing grew. Trees and bushes were barren of leaves, the soil was dry as dust, and even where there were signs of moss and Rot, the deep black had faded to a discoloured ash. Even the air did not feel quite as wet. If the corpse-monuments of what had once been farmlands and meadows did not still stand, all of them could have believed the land was so barren that nothing had ever grown there in the history of the world. Yet it was clear enough that the Rot had been there and was there still, dormant and dreaming, like an undying entity waiting to be awoken.

The ground was bulbous and uneven, and not from lack of taming, but almost tumour-like. The grass, though dead, waved like seaweed on the ocean floor as the chill air whispered through it. The trees and other petrified vegetation twisted skyward in otherworldly shapes that looked more like the tentacled appendages of some horror of the sea than dead, dried foliage. Farren thought about his left hand.

"How did the Church of Areglos keep people away from Stowshaw?" asked Kellen as he looked wide-eyed about the land.

"Sometimes inspiration is more effective than fear," said Farren, trying to forget the ruin of his hand. Kellen looked at him with an inquisitive expression. "The legend of the great Shields of the Church who saved the ill of Stowshaw. What person would venture to a disease-ridden village, when they'd come to revere the Shields' work so much?"

"Well, the Rot came to Kirklyn anyway," said Everett with a hint of mocking in his voice, his head held high. He did not even look at Farren as he said: "So much for the saviours!"

"Why didn't Bram ever go?" said Kellen, continuing his questions despite his muscled companion's scoff.

Farren had never wondered that before. Perhaps Bram didn't know for certain whether it was worth the trip. Certainly, Bram saw the fault with the Church and their serum.

"He was maybe too ill by then," said Farren with a faraway look in his eyes. *The Curse.*

"There are rumours, besides," added Robert. "Some believe that Stowshaw is haunted."

Dayton. The name came to Farren as he stared ahead, like a specter appearing out of the fog. If Robert did not know that much, Farren did. But could he and his heretical band have survived?

"Haunted?" said Kellen. "But what—" But his inquisition was cut off by a raised hand from Jacoby.

They were approaching the top of a small hill in the land and coming over the crest of it, but what was a short hill on their end, tumbled down much steeper and deeper on the opposite end, almost like a cliff. But it was not for the footing that Jacoby motioned for them to halt. Rather, at a fair distance from where the five Reapers stood, upon a flat of land and where the roads from Kirklyn and Stowshaw met, there stood the ruin of an old guard house, long ago abandoned to the dry crumbling of the rest of the land. Its shingled roof had collapsed and it had taken with it part of the rounded walls. Only half of the structure remained standing as a ruined memorial to its original purpose. And wandering aimlessly near the ruin were two misshapen figures that had once been young men, twisted and nearly petrified like the land around them. The two aimless things had some semblance of life in them—or half-life—as they seemingly guarded the road, holding loosely onto or instinctively acting upon the vague memory of their duty.

# V

For a long moment, the five Reapers silently watched the two monstrosities aimlessly circle the ruined guardhouse. Robert and Jacoby crouched down and the others followed. Though so barren was the land near the road to Stowshaw that had the two things looked in the direction of the Reapers, it would not have been difficult to notice them.

"Vernon...and Porter...?" said Robert with a hint of disbelief in his voice, and with that question he spoke to the truth of what they all of them felt.

It was not merely the question of whether or not the two things that stumbled about at a short distance before them were indeed the Twins, but more what exactly was happening to them. All Reapers had at least heard descriptions of what the Curse did to the Old Reapers: the petrification of bone and limb, and the twisting and breaking which took their lives in slow, agonising turns. Then there was also those strange tentacled-worms which Evelyn had described, to the disbelief of all, despite the inhuman physical afflictions of those tainted by the Rot. But here before the five Reapers was a strange amalgam of these two heretofore unlinked things: as though the Twins had been frozen in a state of competing ailments. Farren imagined that not even their mother would be able to tell Porter from Vernon anymore.

From large, barrel-like chests, the legs and arms of the Twins hung—for so vacant did the two seem, that their limbs dangled uselessly from the main husks of their forms, like a sea-creature with wisps of scaled fins floating in the deeps of the ocean. The legs were almost human, but for the uneven way in which the feet stretched out, causing the heels to lift off the ground, creating a hybrid anatomy to that of the legs of a beast of prey. Yet so twisted and half-formed was this transformation that it caused the Twin-things to move with an uneven gait. The only other human feature was the left arm of one of the Twins, which had not elongated to the ground, and instead was twisted and tucked up into its chest.

One of the Twins had a tail-like appendage which grew from the bottom of its spine, whilst the other had two impotent bat wings growing from its back. The tailed Twin only had two spider-leg like stumps where the other's wings were. Both of their heads were elongated, and blissfully one of the Twins managed to have its hood still attached, with a skull-shaped Reaper mask over its face; however, the other Twin's maskless face revealed what horrors might lie beneath its brother's mask. Little indentations had formed in the skull, and from a few of those black, wet eyes blinked from the sockets. Two more of those eyes looked white and blind. This Twin's mouth was stretched across its face, ear to otherwise ear, and that mouth had rows of fangs, sharper than those of a shark.

Otherwise, the Twins were a painful twist of half-living tentacled limbs, bulbous sores, and twisted, almost bark-like skin. They had little scraps of clothing remaining on them—but for the mask of the one brother—and there was a stiffness to their movements, as though the Twins were made of clay that were beginning to dry and harden. It looked like a horrible, painful existence from the outside, and yet the Twins seemed unaware of their condition. Vacuous and soulless, their humanity had long faded.

As Farren looked at the Twins, a cold sweat began to chill his neck and the hairs that still grew thick about his temples. His whole body began to tingle, and he felt a twisting, cold pain in his left hand and the joints of his legs. He choked back bile which pushed up from the pit of his stomach, but he could not keep himself steady and upright. He fell to one side. His mace dropped, as he used his right hand to keep himself from falling flat onto his face.

"Is...this what happened to Oscar...? Is this why Mavis went away?" came Kellen's voice. There was a timbre of trembling in it.

*Bram's Curse.* The thought came to Farren. *But, no. It was more. Was this what the serum did over time? Was it both?* Sweat dappled his forehead, though no-one seemed to notice except:

"You okay, Old Man?" said Jacoby.

Farren looked up at him, and he had the distinct impression Jacoby had been watching him since the attack first seized him. *Was that a hint of a smile? It was not mocking, no. But there was something else there.*

The Old Reaper shook his head and straightened. *It didn't matter. There had to be a cure, and whatever fate had befallen Oscar and Mavis was Evelyn's problem now. Better the bitch to deal with old Mavis. She never shut up about him, the arrogant tw—*

"Two crazed Old Reapers," came Everett's voice cutting through Farren's thought.

"Can we do it?" said Kellen.

"No choice," answered Farren, collecting his thoughts and his mace. "If we're going to pass into Stowshaw, this is the way through."

Without so much as another word, Robert nodded at Farren and with Jacoby and Everett, they descended a short way down the hill and walked wide around where the Twins aimlessly circled, careful to keep as out of sight of the two Old Reapers as possible. Farren sighed, though he could not be certain if he was more pleased to be with Kellen rather than being stuck with Everett. How Robert expected to get the drop on the two with that arrogant cunt with him was beyond Farren.

He and the scrawny Reaper at his side watched as

their three companions circled about the Twins, nearing—though still wide—of the fallen guardhouse below. Then they saw that Jacoby broke off and went a little further round the other side of the ruin. Farren motioned to Kellen and stood.

"C'mon."

As Kellen rose, Farren could already see the apprehension on his face, but there was no time for inspiring words, nor did Farren have a single one to offer. At a light jog, the two began their way down the hill and toward the Twins, Kellen with his axe and long knife, Farren with his spiked mace and shield. Though he wondered how well he could wield the latter as already he felt a twinge of pain in his twisted left hand. He gritted his teeth, but his pace did not slow.

The two Reapers took no caution to go unseen. Quite the contrary. When one of the Twins—the maskless one with the tail—began to turn in the direction of Robert and Everett who crouched just beyond the ruins of the guardhouse in the wilting sward, Farren smashed his mace against his shield as loudly as he could—his brain rung with the pain of each blow.

Both Twins turned toward the sound, and as if to heighten the intention of their march, Kellen drew his long knife along the blade of his axe, slowly and in such a way that sparks flashed from the grating metals, notable enough under the overcast sky. It seemed to dazzle the Twins for a moment; or at least to keep their attention fixed forward. Then, as though in answer, the maskless one stiffened and let out a half-human cry from its hideous maw. The other twin stood silent, or seemingly so, with tentacled appendages twitching greedily.

Then, as the maskless twin began to move toward the two Reapers, bounding along the dirt and kicking up dust as it went, Farren saw Kellen duck, his weapons held out on either side of him, as the scrawny Reaper rushed forward like harsh winds through a wheat field.

*So the young one did have some courage, after all.* Farren couldn't help but smile despite the oncoming threat.

Kellen reached the horror first, ducking swiftly around the elongated arms that lashed out at him, and even as he moved, Kellen swung his knife and axe so that he chopped and sliced in the same motion. The Twin, likely unused to pain having stood so long unchallenged in that place, staggered back and let out a hideous cry. Though Farren was shocked to see the monstrosity was so quick on the recovery. He wondered if Kellen had really pierced the thing's flesh or not, and fortunately for Kellen, Farren had nearly caught up.

Just as Kellen was strafing the thing and as the Twin was so quick on the recovery, it began to swing its tail-like appendage directly at Kellen. Farren lept into the air, still on a downward slope of the land, and with his weapons raised, pushed off toward the creature. With recognition of a threat, the thing saw Farren, but just a moment too late.

With a crunch, Farren drove his shield into the face of the creature. Pain seared through Farren's joints, and his knees nearly buckled as he hit the ground. The force was enough to knock the creature slightly off balance. Farren saw from the corner of his eye that Kellen still took a hit from the tail, but it only dropped him to his knee for a moment before the young scarecrow was back on the attack. Farren, despite the pain in his left hand, did not let up on his flurry of attacks either.

Even as his heavy boots met the ground, Farren used the momentum of his own near-fall to bring his mace upward in a second blow to the thing's face. The blow did some work toward staggering the creature for a second time, but despite the burst of black blood which clouded the air for a moment, no real damage seemed to be done to the thing. When Farren brought his third strike down, this one too with his mace, he had the distinct feeling the weapon did little damage at all—no more than had he taken a feather to a stone.

Kellen, he saw too, was not having much better luck. Even the slicing cuts of the scarecrow Reaper's long blade were doing little to injure the creature. The cuts did not draw blood or otherwise create a wound. But the two men fought on—there was little other choice now.

As Farren lunged forward with his shield again, focused forward on the threat before him, he registered the slower, but oncoming threat of the second, hooded twin, but the thing had not come far enough to help its brother when out rushed Everett and Robert. With a great yell, Everett warned the hooded twin of the oncoming blow of his great hammer. *Fool*, thought Farren as his shield smashed into the neck of the maskless twin. *Still not enough.*

Everett's strike missed as the hooded twin wriggled backward, the large hammer smashing only dirt and rock. But Robert was fast on the attack. He lept forward, shotels in hand and with one he hooked an oncoming tentacle from the twin's body as he slipped to one side of it, yet when he brought the second weapon down, it barely made a mark in the creature's flesh.

His blood froze.

Farren most of all that crew was familiar with the Rot-soaked mess of battle against those driven insane by the Rot, though the others had seen their small share of combat—if you could call the early massacres combat. Though dangerous because of the sheer unchecked violence of them, especially when in large numbers, those infected by the Lunatic Rot fell like any other man would to the weapons of the Reapers. But these things, twisted differently than the sacks which grew in place of the Infected's heads, did not seem to feel their blows any more than a playful slap from a hand wrapped in a well-padded glove. But this was no sport, despite the bloody joy the Reapers once felt in their work. Only the smell was the same: the stench of choking, foetid rot.

As the stink permeated all his senses and the pain shot through his arm, Farren could feel his resolve falter. The insane, inhuman creature moved so much faster than he expected from something so horrifically twisted and stiff. It had little trouble dealing with the two Reapers at once. A flail of its elongated arms and tentacles swept through the air, forcing both Kellen and Farren to dodge out of the way. And though Farren could see even light-equipped Kellen was losing stamina and ground, Farren still more was finding it difficult to counter the flurry of wild attacks coming from the blasphemous fiend.

The thing screeched again, and Farren fell back. It

was like a slash of red through the back of his eyes. A ringing started in his ears. He was vaguely aware of Kellen still fighting, seemingly unaffected by the cry of that thing. Farren rose to his feet, lifting his mace for an attack, but a falling limb was coming at him faster still. He felt his knees begin to stiffen with that growing familiar sensation. *Not now.* He heard a cry. *Everett. Fool.* The limb came down. Farren was forced to raise his shield. He had no other choice. The tentacled limb smashed down with a dull thud. His arm stuck. It would not move, and the pain that came with the paralysis was unbearable.

He reeled. His companion cried out a word. *Farren!* His name. Blade and axe bounced from the thing's hide. Away he saw a giant of a man being crushed by some tentacled creature. Bones crunching. Another blow. His shield dropped. His eyes blurred, but with some strange blood-like liquid, moving through his vision as though staining in his eyeballs. He stumbled. Or did he move at all? He could not move. He could barely see. More screams. The smell of Rot. Ringing. Stiff petrification. Pain. A splash of black blood. Curse.

And then all went black.

# VI

"No. Just give him a moment."

He felt he would vomit. His stomach turned. All the world came dizzyingly back to him. That voice. "See?"

Slowly he opened his eyes. A gloved hand came into

view. He looked up, and it was like looking into the Sun. *It had come back.* He had lived to see it again. *No. That was not the Sun. Something else.* He couldn't quite make it out. He squinted. The smell of incense nearly choked him. *That wasn't frankincense.* And that strange symbol. Just there on the wrist.

Farren brushed the hand away lightly with a grunt. Slowly he rose to his feet. He still clenched his mace tightly in his right hand. *My shield.* He looked up and saw Kellen holding it. Robert and Jacoby were standing over him as well. Farren's limbs were so stiff. There wasn't pain now, but the resistance felt like trying to bend a thick, live tree branch. He let out a deep sigh as slowly he felt his limbs loosen.

"It was bloody work," said Robert. "We thought we'd lost you too."

Kellen returned Farren's shield to him. The stiffness in his left hand was still quite severe, but slowly it was dissipating. Though Farren hardly noticed. He saw the fallen creature, its elongated head severed from its twisted form. His eyes wandered then to the ruin of the guardhouse and near to it was a heap of tentacles and flesh. It almost looked like the meat on a butcher's table. Black blood with ribbons of red running through it. Twisted in the pile of tentacles and flesh was a modified sallet and a great hammer.

*What a fecking moron. Too young. Too ambitious. Like Evelyn.*

"It took some work to get through their hides, but we managed. Though Jacoby wins the day," said Robert. "He managed the deathblow to both."

Farren turned to look at Jacoby. There was a slight smirk playing on his lips as he looked back at Farren. "Are you okay, Old Man?" That question was beginning to irritate him. He nodded, shortly and stiffly.

"If what we've learned is true," continued Robert. "Vernon and Porter were the last of our concerns. No one else was sent to Stowshaw, and its no secret that Orianna and Mortimer were long taken care of. If there is knowledge to find in Stowshaw, the Twins should have been our last barrier."

*Unless Dayton survived.* He and his merry men had done as much damage as the Infected when Stowshaw was lost and abandoned.

"Let's just hope the others are successful too," said Kellen. He looked at the ruin near the guardhouse. "There's more danger in Kirklyn."

Jacoby smiled again, but to Farren it did not seem encouraging despite his words: "I'm certain there are answers to find in Stowshaw."

Farren's eyes narrowed. *A cure?*

He looked down at the twisted corpse of the nearer twin. He felt unconscious movement in his left hand. A pain and a stiffening. But he held to his shield tight and to his consciousness, though a momentary flash of red cut through his vision.

"Let's hope you're right," Farren said, unable to help but partially betray his thoughts. He wondered then if perhaps the Twins had managed to keep a store of serum there in that guardhouse. Though fallen to ruin, perhaps at least one vial had remained unbroken. What Farren wouldn't give to have some of that serum now: it's healing properties, the sense of boundless energy it gave, and a relief from the pain of the Curse. *Just what had the Church used to create it?* The Church Reapers and the Shields before them had referred to it as a sort of Communion, and it was only supposed to be taken during worship and rituals, though plenty of Church Reapers were able to smuggle vials of it out from the storehouses in Areglos. But the substance did not taste like wine, nor like blood. *Something strange to the palate. It would be so helpful to have some just now.*

"Hi! Farren!" came Kellen's voice through the fog. Farren looked back, and he suddenly realised he had stepped toward the guardhouse. Kellen was nearby enough, but Robert and Jacoby had already moved ahead on the road. Farren just shook his head, and joined Kellen as they followed the other two Reapers. Though Farren had the distinct impression Jacoby had looked backward once or twice as Farren shook off his daze.

# VII

As the four Reapers continued through the half fog, the sun moved, obscured, through the aether. The sun was bright enough and the fog light enough that they could trace its arc as it moved to a position in the sky just in front of them, and until it became partially obscured by the vague shapes of rooftops and a great wall.

Even in the uneven light they could see how dry the land had become. The soil beneath their feet felt almost like sand, and if the wind blew, dust kicked up into the air—enough to choke them had it not been for their masks. No grass grew there, and the trees and plants they passed looked as though they had been sculpted from ash. There was a horrible smell in the air. An old smell. A smell of dried rot and decay.

Nothing else moved within their vision other than the shifting fog itself, and there was no sound but for the soft crunch of their boots. Even the wind did not whisper. It was as though the very essence of the land and sky above it had been sucked dry. It was hard to imagine anything ever had lived there or could ever sustain itself in that land again. Farren began to doubt the purpose of coming to Stowshaw and even more now that any hint of a cure could be found. If that were the case, he would rather they were quick about it all. He did not care to die in such a waste. He could feel his joints twist and tighten, and in his head and hand began a dull throb.

Within the ever-shifting mists, it seemed they came rather suddenly upon the half-decayed wooden walls of abandoned Stowshaw. The old town was so silent and ruined it looked so much older than the town actually was. It had been only twenty years since the horrors of Stowshaw and the outbreak of the Rot there, and yet time had passed like ages there.

The tall wooden wall which had one time surrounded the entirety of the village, sunk and fell in places, and great holes gaped in the stout boards, giving the impression of the hollowed, rotten trees. Looking through the holes and as they stepped through beyond the falling barrier, the company of Reapers saw that the town was in no better shape than the wall that contained it. They caught their breath as they looked upon the impossibly leaning buildings, the sag of roofs, the maddening chaos of it all. The very place and all aspects of it seemed to defy all laws of nature, and had those men not seen the things they had already seen throughout the Rot's spread, this sight may indeed have broken them. Instead, each one individually thought of Kirklyn, and they knew then that as dire as the situation there had become, it could get so much worse.

Farren felt a cold sweat on his forehead, which stung in the still, dry air. He felt again the painful twisting of his joints and could feel his consciousness slipping. Shots of red darted through his vision. A ringing sound clouded his hearing. He could taste and smell the foetid stench of rot. His head felt as though it were tossed into the ocean on a cloudy day, and he nearly stumbled to one side. He felt beneath his palm the touch of dry, splintered wood. He choked back an acrid bile. A nauseating weakness stole through his body, and he grunted as sharp, twisting pains washed away the sick. His vision, blurred, began to return. He blinked. Jacoby was staring at him.

"The chapel should be the first place to check," Farren managed and forced himself to step forward. His legs did not want to move, and he clapped Kellen hard on the shoulder. It was a feigned act of affectionate encouragement, disguising his need of support for a moment. Kellen smiled at the Old Reaper. It seemed Kellen had taken no notice of his spell, *but what of Jacoby?*

"I wonder if any of those lunatics survived," said

Kellen, looking now at the others. Farren noticed a twitch in Jacoby's eye.

"They aren't lunatics," Jacoby answered, and there was a touch of...*is that anger in his voice?* If so, he quickly disguised it as he continued. "The people of Stowshaw, they were innocent of the horrors brought upon them. Sick, infected, poor. Show more respect."

Kellen gulped hard, but spoke not another word, nor did any of them as Robert led them into the town proper and toward the still discernible, half-standing rood which stood from the peak of the chapel's dome, still some distance away upon the hill about the center of town. It was a symbol of their old faith—something they believed older than the land itself—but what was it now? The Church Reapers and their Communion of the Holy Serum. The sermons heard in the Grand Cathedral. Something had changed since Stowshaw. The younger amongst them did not even know the old prayers. Were they even still worshiping the same god in Kirklyn? There were rumours, but the Church of Argelos never made any official decree to that effect.

As before, there were no sounds heard within the town and nothing—even the air—moved. They all felt they would choke on the silence, and their ears were pricked for any sound. Farren could feel his jaw tighten, his teeth grinding as he flexed his fingers upon his mace and shield. His left hand especially was becoming tight. He could feel a soreness around his ears where they met his skull. His breathing, however, he kept calm as well as he could, and he did not think he could hear the breath of the others. They all looked tense, walking at a cautious, determined pace toward the center hill, their heads darting from side to side, their bodies slightly hunched as though ready for combat at any moment. Or rather, Farren noticed they both walked as such—Kellen and Robert, that is. There was something more casual about Jacoby's gait, and Farren had not noticed before that the man's sword was not even drawn. *As bad as Everett,* he thought, *killed two Old Reapers and now you get careless.*

To the Reapers, the walk to the chapel seemed endless, past the gaping, blackened voids of doors and windows. The way in which the architecture twisted and sagged, the homes and abandoned establishments, they looked more like the melting skulls of inhuman horrors than they did the workmanship of Man. A blasphemous mockery of their former use, now disregarded headstones of a people none would mourn.

Farren could feel himself dizzying again, and he tried to shake it off. He nearly stumbled once more when a voice righted him.

"Psst!" Kellen whispered, twisting his head as though to look back over his shoulder, though the lanky, seemingly nervous Reaper never took his eyes from the ruins that loomed up around them. "Farren. Were you here? Did you fight in this battle?"

The pain twisted in his arm. A flash of red went through Farren's vision again. He twisted his head to one side and squinted his eyes.

"Hey, Farren. Old man?"

"Damn it!" Farren burst out, gritting his teeth from the pain of his condition, and Kellen's questions were doing nothing toward making it better. "How fecking old d'you think I am?!"

A hiss came from Robert. He motioned for the two to keep silent. Jacoby was watching him again, but Farren did not care for the moment. His mind was on the Curse. Certainly, he wasn't quite old enough to have fought in the battles to quell the plague in Stowshaw, but he was old enough to have known the men who did. Old enough to have trained with them. Old enough to have tasted the Church's serum but a few times. It seemed that was enough. Old Bram was right. *Damn him and his fecking Curse!*

The red flashed once more, and Farren this time let out a grunt. It felt as though his whole body throbbed. His ribs stiffened like a vice was closing on his organs, and his left arm cramped and twisted so that the shield fell from his fingers with a clang against the gravel street. Kellen cried out and went to assist the Old Reaper, and again came the hissing call for silence from Robert, but over the din came the distant sound of something else: something like a scream, but it did not sound quite human.

The three Reapers looked up at the vacant homes, gaping blackly at them in horror as though they had been the ones to scream. Farren however did not hear so much as feel the scream. His veins pulsed hot with blood.

"Get the feck off me!" He yelled, and Kellen drew back, wide-eyed. Jacoby turned toward Farren, watching him, and seeming unfazed by the outburst. Robert continued to look at the leaning architecture, his sword raised. Another cry came, and this one was closer now.

Farren fell to his knees, his head twisting to one side, stuck there in a nigh impossible twist. His body began to rock and shake. He could not see for the blood-cloud before his eyes. But he could taste—taste the sweetly fragrant rot which floated through the air all about him, masking even the sickening scent of incense nearby.

The others could smell it too—the Rot—but to them it did not taste so sweet as it assailed their senses. Only Jacoby seemed relatively unaffected, either way, as he continued to watch Farren seizure on the ground. Farren tried to shake off the fit and gain some semblance of control. He breathed deep and stood, but the smell of the Rot drove him wild. He shook his head. The mists half cleared from his vision—enough to see that from the gaping, black holes within the dreaded heap of brick and wood around them, swarms of Infected crawled out into the street, surrounding the four companions.

# VIII

The Infected did not utter a sound as they poured out from the black void of the ruined town, but from their swollen, sack-like heads came a sickening swishing and gurgling, as of liquid bubbling and tossing within their gross heads. With those sounds, there also was movement—like a child moving within a mother's womb, only more pronounced, and just like a woman's stomach in the late days of pregnancy, the heads of these Infected looked fit to burst.

"How did their heads not explode in all this time?" whispered Kellen, barely audible through his dry, half-choked throat. Wide-eyed the scarecrow-like Reaper gripped his long knife and axe as he watched the infected horde slowly close in around them.

"They could be new," said Robert twirling his shotels anxiously. "The Twins couldn't have watched the perimeter perfectly since being assigned to guard here."

"So many..." came Kellen's voice.

"Or—" but Jacoby was unable to finish that statement. With a sudden burst of insane, unchecked frenzy, the entire crowd of Infected rushed in toward the four Reapers. With a howl, Farren rose to his feet, smashing a shoulder up into the chest of one of the oncoming things and bringing his mace down upon its head, splashing a burst of blood and bone into the air. But rather than acrid iron, the wound smelled of tainted rot—a smell which seemed now to drive the Old Reaper mad with the thrill of battle and slaughter. That alone, perhaps, is what saved him from succumbing to the pain surging through his body.

He barely took note that Jacoby had no time to pull out his weapons before the man was lost in the sea of the Rot infected lunatics that clawed and tore recklessly at the Reapers, as heads burst and more infected came out of the darkness around them. Not six of the infected were slain between them before Farren saw Robert slip on the viscera from one of the fallen infected's heads. He let drop one of his shotels to catch his balance as another of the terrific horde seized on him, spinning its claw-like hands in a deadly whirlwind.

Robert, seeing the danger he was in, brought up his armoured arm to quickly shield himself as he attempted to regain his footing, but the flurry of strikes were too fast, even for the well-trained Reaper, and the ground too wet with goo. Just as he blocked two more slashes, his legs slid again, and the third tore straight through Robert's throat, sending breath, blood and soul into the night sky.

Farren heard Kellen cry out for Robert and rush forward to slay his companion's murderer, but so blood-drunk was Farren, so lost in the red mist and the smell of Rot, that could he barely feel the sting of the raking blows that managed to break through the smash of his weapon. It was some fixation and obsessive drive that guided his mace, blow after blow. It felt like the old days, after he had first been offered the Church's serum and went out Reaping the Infected in the worst plagued spots in Kirklyn. Oh, the glory! The cool splash of blackish, infected blood. The satisfying squish of a well-landed hit. The smell of Rot.

But the berserk mood did not last, and red began again to flash before his eyes—eyes that then cleared enough to see the slashing claw of an Infected reach out through the red mist. Instinctively Farren lifted his hand to ward off this unwanted touch. The claws tore through his glove, shredding the open palm of his twisted hand. Such was the pain in that moment that, in a sudden burst of clarity, the mists cleared the red at last subsided. Farren's arm twisted and cramped again, and his hand tucked against his chest, pinned there uselessly. He remembered the Twins. Farren twisted around, gritting his teeth as his mace smashed through his attacker's sack-like head, bursting with a squelch as he half dragged the corpse around with the swing of his arm.

There was a momentary break in the assault, for a great number of the Infected had managed to overwhelm Kellen, even as he slashed and slayed his enemies. His axe sunk deep into the sack and neck of an infected, but he was not able to retrieve it as two more closed in, slashing at that forearm and shoulder. The scarecrow-like Reaper cried out as even more came upon him, slashing, tearing, and clawing the man to shreds of cloth and skin. Farren's blood ran cold and a chill sweat was on his neck and dappled his thinning hair as he watched the inhuman pulpy mass come apart in the hands of those fiends.

"Farren!"

The pain in his arm made him wince. It was the only thing that kept tears from starting in his eyes and the sick from shredding up from his stomach.

"Hi! Farren!"

But there was no mouth or throat left upon the bloody heap that had once been Kellen.

"Farren!"

The call was loud and clear. Just beyond the horde ripping mindlessly at the fleshy horror stood the church. Farren had not even realised they had come so close to it, and there standing on the steps was Jacoby, waving him onward. An odd light seemed to radiate from the Reaper—thought it was not a light in the truest sense. It was something else that made it difficult for Farren to focus on the man, but he saw it was indeed Jacoby, and there were no infected near him.

Already the crowd was becoming bored with shredding at the scraps upon the gravel, and two turned toward Farren. His arm was still in immense pain, but he heaved himself up, simultaneously swinging his mace into the sacky head of the foremost infected. As it fell, he pushed forward, half hobbling as he drove his shoulder into the body of the thing, sending it stumbling back into the second oncoming threat. Others were already rushing toward him, and he spun once to dash the innards of one more inhuman thing into the air.

He barely gained the steps of the church, when one of the Infected, two steps behind him, slashed into the back of Farren's thigh, and the Old Reaper brought his mace down into the thing's fleshy head. As it sprawled backward, some of the others tripped over the body, one of which burst upon the steps as it came forward. Farren wasted no time. He raced up the remaining steps as best he could and gained the half-fallen church doors.

He threw himself through the doors, and smashed his back against them with all his weight and force, managing to shut them against the oncoming infected, despite the state of disrepair of the doors. He closed his eyes for but a moment, allowing himself three deep breaths as the twisting pain in his arm throbbed, and the red flashes again throbbed at the back of his eyes. Then he opened them and looked about.

He saw that his refuge was too exposed. The battles of Stowshaw had reduced the place to a ruin, and gaping holes in the walls and windows offered multiple entries into the sanctuary. Whatever respite and protection

Farren had hoped for in that holy monument, there was none, and already the Infected were making their way through the holes in the chapel's walls.

He swore, gritted his teeth. His hand tightened on his mace. Yet as he watched hopeless, prepared to make the best end he could—and pushing back the horrors his mind conjured up of the true, visceral experience of that end—his glance fell upon the dais at the far side of the chapel. There stood Jacoby, waving Farren on again.

The Old Reaper blinked away another red flash, and he saw the other Reaper disappear from view as though he sunk into the very stone of the floor. Farren began to wonder if Jacoby were not merely some ghost conjured up by his half-mad brain, but he ran forward all the same, as more and more of the Infected climbed into the church and ran toward him.

His left arm bent and twisted in impossible directions, as though the very bones were made of liquid in his skin. The sensation brought more red flashes and half-focused visions. His knees tensed and swelled with petrification. His stomach lurched into his throat, but he swallowed back the bile and ran.

As he came up the three steps of the dais, the Infected closed behind him, Farren saw that the altar had been pushed back somewhat, revealing a great gaping black pit of impenetrable dark and a series of stairs which led down into it. Without thinking, Farren stumbled forward and down the stairs, ignoring the pain and the red flashes. Then, once more, the dark became absolute.

# IX

A dull, dizzying throb began to beat against his skull. His stomach gurgled and twisted. Red flashed against the blackness. He blinked, but all was dark. The pain had subsided in his left arm, but he could barely move it. *Had I passed out?* Farren wondered. *Perhaps.* There was no sound above or around him. His back was against a hard surface. His legs were under him. He reached out with his right hand, searching for his mace, but his hand only felt cool, hard stone to the side of him, and once or twice the clacking, light, hard and dry surface of something that had once breathed with life.

*So, the tales were true, then.*

Recognising the futility of his efforts in such complete darkness, Farren gave up the search for his mace, but the Old Reaper knew it would do him no good to merely sit there and wait for someone to find him. No one else was coming to Stowshaw—that was not in any part of the remaining Reapers' plans. Curse his foolishness for hoping to find a cure here. Now Bram's Curse was like to take him in the miserable silence amongst the dead, sleeping beneath the Infected.

Another flash of red, and the pain began to steal up his left arm from his forearm to his shoulder. His hand had no feeling at all, pinned there against his stomach.

Farren grit his teeth and slowly pushed himself to his feet. He used the wall to keep himself from going back down. His legs were so stiff. No surprise. He could feel they were petrifying, following his now useless left arm. But he was an Old Reaper, and they weren't the sort to meet their fate lying down in the dark. It wasn't in their blood.

*Blood. Serum. Bram's Curse.*

When Farren gained his feet, he let out a grunt with a last effort that ended in a sigh. A soft echo called back to him and followed by a second sound—tapping of some sort. His hearing was clouded, and his balding head beading with sweat. It was the first moment he realised his hood was off. He braced himself against the wall with his right hand and caught his breath. When he was steady again, he tore himself free of his mask. He no longer saw the purpose in its protection. Not for him, and not down there. He let out another sigh. The tapping came again. His head throbbed and then he turned his head away and shut his eyes as light came into his world again.

It was only a dull, sickly light, but in such complete darkness it was like a sudden flare of the Sun. Farren blinked and blinked again. The dull throb remained in his head, but he adjusted to the light enough to keep his eyes open.

Faraway the light flickered and sputtered its orange glow against the choking black. Farren could not see its source, but it must have been of a fire by the way it moved. Between he and it, Farren saw what he had already guessed: stone walls, floors, and an arched ceiling, and deep grooves all along the walls filled with bones— all human by the look of them and long browned by the slow decay of ages uncounted. Some had fallen to the floor around him, but there was no sight of his mace. He looked back toward the staircase but there was none there.

*Where am I?*

He swooned and caught the wall again with a grunt, and then came the voice.

"Ah, Farren! So, you're awake. I want you to see something. Hurry. Ere the night takes you forever."

*Jacoby.*

So, it wasn't a phantom which led him here— wherever here was. There were tales that the old seat of Areglos had been in Stowshaw before moving to Kirklyn, and that countless deacons, vicars, and bishops had been placed in the catacombs beneath the chapel here, for countless generations and even after the Grand Cathedral of the Church of Areglos in Kirklyn had been erected—all until the Rot took Showshaw. And there were other rumours too about those tombs, but not even Mavis or Bram had known for certain what amount of truth inspired them. That was why they were sent here to investigate. But this place…

Farren looked again at the bones and the stones built around them. They were incredibly ancient, the bones half rotted away, and he saw to his horror what he had not noted at first: that these bones were somewhat larger than human bones—though they looked human enough—and that the stones around them were carved with strange hieroglyphs and symbols that were of no language he knew. Not even in faraway villages like Hamming, where people still kept a semblance of their more ancient tongue, did such symbols exist. Even more, Farren wondered, *how did Jacoby know this was here to show him anything?*

Farren grit his teeth and began to move forward,

clutching to the wall as he half dragged his stiff, petrified legs along the floor. Whatever Jacoby was about, Farren meant to find out. He had his suspicions now, and though he did not like it, nor had he ever been in Stowshaw before, one thing was whispered amongst the oldest of the Reapers that none but maybe the highest members of the Church of Areglos knew: that when the Shields of the Church came to Stowshaw to stop the spread of the Rot, they were hunted and attacked by a group believed to be led by the Heretic Dayton. Farren's blood boiled as he thought of how few of the Church Reapers had returned from Stowshaw. Sweat trickled down his head, and the stiffness of his legs came in throbs as they began to loosen. He began to move faster, limping along at a good pace and gritting through the pain. The dull throb continued in his head, and every now and then he would stumble as red slashed through his vision. The Curse was doing its work, but not before Farren got to Jacoby. He was determined on that point.

At the end of the first long, necrotic hall, Farren saw the way split and from his left came a fluttering light as from a torch. Just as it caught his eye, he saw the form of Jacoby turn down another hall, torch in hand and leaving the hall in partial darkness again. He could smell a strange sent; not Rot or decay or dry, stale earth, but another, more otherwise calming scent. An incense—but it was not frankincense. The cold sweat on his head stung, and he grunted and yelled to the elusive man as he threw himself across the open floor where the halls split and grabbed hold of the ledge of one of the crypt's shelves.

"Come on, Old Man! There isn't much time left, and I don't want you to miss this."

Farren was already on the move and had gained the end of the next hall in time to see torch and man turn yet another corner. Farren kept up, but it was no easy going for him. The throbbing in his head made it difficult to see and concentrate. The red flashes and fallen bones caused him to stumble. The pain and petrification made movement near impossible, but Farren was trained by the old ways. He was a hard man. He went on, corridor after corridor through the maze-like necropolis. At some point he forgot even the maze and lost all sense of direction, as it all blended into a single, dizzying chase for that torch. But at long last Farren turned a corner into a short hall, and he saw that the torch had cornered itself in a chamber just at the far end of a short hall.

The red flashes continued, flickering when they did. Farren felt as though he would wretch. The throbbing in his head became intense again, yet he pushed on slowly toward the opened chamber, though something about the room seemed to repel him. He heard Jacoby's voice again from within, but he could not quite make it out. Instead, his attention seemed inexplicably drawn to the shattered wooden doors of the chamber. They were not made with any wood of the world he knew. Almost alien they seemed, but he knew indeed the substance was wood. Like the catacomb stones, the doors had all sorts of strange, unknowable symbols upon them. But one symbol in particular stood out: a strange rune carved and filled with some golden-copper substance. The rune had the abstract shape of a man hanging upside down—at least Farren thought that is what he saw at times. It was difficult to focus on, as at certain angles it seemed almost to burn bright like the Sun. A wrist, the thought to came to him. Something about a wrist. The scent of lavender was suddenly recognisable to him.

In a nauseated fog, he stumbled determinedly though the door, and into the vast chamber. Three large steps lead down from the door and to an uneven stone floor, in the center of which, two steps up, was an altar of sorts. The walls and high-vaulted ceiling were made of the same stone—dark and otherworldly, like the bricks of the catacombs behind him. Yet unlike the catacombs, here and there were beams and boxes and tall slats along the walls made with the same wooden substance as that from which the doors was fashioned. And like the doors, these pieces of wood had the same golden-copper substance laid in it, fashioned into the same strange abstract symbol of a hanging man.

Farren fell forward. His legs completely stiffened for a moment, and he toppled down the stone steps with a hard crash to the stone floor. He grunted and a cough tore through his throat. He felt dry, parched even, as though all the moisture were sucked from his body. A flecks black came out with the cough. Something was stabbing at his back, and he rolled over to see a broken, dried root poking through the uneven floor—it looked as old and ancient as the bones within the catacombs. Then Farren looked about and he saw the place was filled with dried roots and clumps of a black and grey powdery substance, as though mold—long dried—had once grown there. It occurred to him then how inexplicably dry that ancient necrohol was, especially considering how deep below ground Farren guessed he was. He looked up, and to his horror, he saw, hanging down like thousands of jellyfish below the ocean's depths, dried roots hung from the ceiling—also ancient and long dead.

*What is this place?*

Wide-eyed he looked more closely upon the boxes along the walls and saw that strange twisting shapes peeked from under some of the lids—like the mummified tentacles of unnameable creatures. Farren's thoughts immediately went to the Twins who guarded Stowshaw and other terrible sightings men and women had died raving about back in Kirklyn. Something only Evelyn had claimed to see. But when Farren's eyes landed on one of the symbols again, he curled up with a vicious pain in his head, and the red flashes came in excruciating bursts. He could not even feel his left arm anymore, but his legs twisted in agony.

Farren squinted his eyes and crawled toward the center of the chamber, barely making much progress, until the pain subsided enough that with a tremendous effort and cry, he got to his feet. His legs were barely of any use now, but he managed to half-throw himself up the steps to the stone altar where he hoped to gain his balance once more. But when the Old Reaper caught the edge of the stone altar and he looked down, the still human part of him reeled with insanity.

For the altar was no altar at all, but a stone coffin, the lid thrown back and to the ground behind it. It was long and wide and lined with the same strange wood as the boxes and door leading into the chamber. Along the wood's edges, the golden-copper symbol was set in a repeating pattern of even spacing—or so Farren assumed because they were half obscured by the mummified horror of what looked to be a tall, thin man.

Like the bones beyond the chamber, this body was human-like, but not human. It was some other thing from a time more ancient than any tales he had ever heard—even as a child in the nursery. Long white hair grew from the thing's temples below an oddly shaped crown made of that same strange metal of golden-copper, and it wore long robes that Farren could see despite their greyed and rotted appearance were like to have once been as gaudy and lavish of any king or bishop among men. The real horror of the thing, however, was not in its suggestion of ancient and unknowable aeons, but in the visible transformation which undoubtedly this ruler had undergone before and even as he died.

The King's legs were twisted in grotesque ways, and it seemed, by the bulges beneath his robes, that other like-limbs were growing around his waist. His face, eyes hollow and open as though in horror, twisted on the left side, pulling the dried skin almost in a curl, and the hair on that side had begun to take on a thicker, more sentient aspect—indeed the hairs lay twisted like tentacled roots on that side of the King's head. The King's right hand seemed untouched by the terrifying metamorphosis and rested against his waist, palm toward his head, as though he had been holding something there that had been taken from him after death. The left hand was in like position, but it was no true hand that stood opposite the right, but instead a twisting tangle of fingers-turned-short-tentacles. Farren looked down at his own left hand and saw there the similarities.

His brain reeled again, and his legs failed him. He caught the side of the abhorred sarcophagus and slid down it. He now faced the doors through which he had come. The red flashed and flickered. His head throbbed. Black once more flecked the air as he coughed dry and painfully. The skin around his eyes were sore, but he managed to open them and shake away the red mist when he heard the sound of boots clopping on stone from somewhere behind him. And he could smell the stench of lavender incense.

"Bram's Curse. That's what you call it, you Reapers, do you not?"

Farren's mind reeled. His eyes felt heavy, but the Old Reaper fought for consciousness. The slow footfalls of booted feet approached.

"The slow, twisting death of those who once imbibed the blood of the Nameless One, but gave up that Communion."

At last Jacoby clopped into view before the Old Reaper, standing on the uneven floor below the steps up to the Dried King's coffin. It was difficult to focus on Jacoby—especially on his wrist, but Farren could faintly make out a bracelet made of strange wood and fixed with a golden-copper symbol. Farren smiled.

"It was found here, in this very chamber, in the arms of that very king whose name is lost to time. We call them the Lunaerians, for it appears they worshiped the moon, in the long dark past, but the Nameless One—whatever It is—came from the stars and fell into the sea and somehow these Lunaerians called It up. For a time, they worshiped It, and under that worship, they flourished—until they learned the truth: that It is some malicious force, symbiotic and parasitic. Those whom commune with It become one with It, and those who do not become its prey, infected by an insane metamorphosis that allows them to be harvested for Its food. And so, It grows more powerful and spreads.

"At least, this is the best we have been able to interpret from the writings of these Lunaerians—what little we can—and from watching and documenting. And watched we have, for a long time, from the shadows."

Farren's consciousness was fading fast. It was becoming difficult to focus on what Jacoby was saying, but he heard enough, and a name came back to him which now he spoke aloud:

"Dayton."

"Died some years ago," said Jacoby. "Branded a heretic by the Church of Areglos for refusing communion with the Nameless One and cast out, but not before learning the significance of this strange wood and symbol. Inquisitor Gervaise, amongst the first to partake of the Nameless One's flesh with Orianna and Mallory, lost his arm when it was stabbed with a splinter from the box which held It entombed here, secret, and safe, for ages.

"Thus, we wear the symbol on our persons, us Watchers, and we fashion our weapons with it. For the Body seems to give visions and knowledge beyond human scope, and the Blood an inhuman physicality. If only we could know why. Dayton left us the sacred texts of the Lunaerians to attempt to translate and what knowledge he had. I'm confi—"

But Jacoby's speech was interrupted by a dry, hoarse laugh from Farren. Jacoby frowned and his eyes widened manically.

"A bunch of lost boys playing at swords." He laughed harder now—*they didn't know any more than the Reapers*—but the humorous thought was cut off by a harsh coughing. Farren vomited up thick, black blood. Pain shot through his undulating stomach, and the red flashed before his eyes—or rather, his vision flashed through the red.

"I could see you were experiencing the withdrawals," Jacoby continued. "You'll die anyway. Dayton's Watchers only care to heal the innocent infected, not those who have taken of the Nameless One. But when you made it this far, I didn't have the heart to let you die without knowing you died upholding the hideous crimes of men who only cared for their own gain—men who too would have died as the Lunaerian King."

The thought occurred to Farren that it was a sympathetic turn which motivated Jacoby's incessant prattling. Farren only wished Jacoby would come close so that he could get his fingers on him as they petrified around the youthful traitor's throat. But Jacoby barely moved from his spot and Farren was no longer certain he could lift even his unafflicted arm.

Dayton's Watcher went on with his monologue, but Farren could catch so little of what was said. Just words. *Mavis. Mallory. The Old Reapers. The Infected. Areglos.* It was all in a haze of muffled sound, stabbing pains, and flashes of red. Then clarity came again for a moment, and through a red fog he heard, almost far away, Jacoby's voice:

"We have men all over, and not just in Kirklyn. We will fulfill Dayton's commitment to stop the spread of this plague and cure the Infected. A true holy man of Areglos. None will leave Kirklyn who are not brought here to Stowshaw to await the cure. Even now we have other Watchers among you Reapers, and stationed beyond Kirklyn's borders...there is a man just now..."

But Farren's consciousness began to fade again, and Jacoby's voice quieted into muffled nothings. The red fog turned brownish green and then black. He felt so dry, like everything was being sapped from his body. *Serum.* He needed serum.

And then he heard it, clear as any sound he had heard in the waking world. But was he not awake, alive? *A cure.* He came for a cure. But how could he hear that sound so far away, here in the deepest regions of the Earth? And yet he heard it: the clear, hollow, resonant bells of Areglos.

*Evelyn!* the thought came.

*Did she succeed?*

And he knew no more.

From
*ROBERT PHILIPS*
Also by J. M. DeSantis

# PROLOGUE

It is with a considerable amount of apprehension that I so much as recall the tale of Robert Phillips, even so many years after his disappearance—despite what the authorities say on the matter.

The reasons for such feelings have nothing whatever to do with the man named here. For a good portion of the time I knew him, Robert was well-reasoning and kind, even if eccentric. Even after that strange madness seemed to take hold of him, I still felt nothing but amiably toward and genuinely concerned for my friend.

Rather, it is the very nature of his disappearance, the events which led up to it, the horrifying thing I believe that I witnessed, and the hideous truths I have since learned which has driven me to the sorry state I now find myself in: no longer a respected professor of History and searching obsessively for any remaining copy of an old and forbidden grimoire in order that I might destroy it, and being hunted unceasingly by members of the cults who follow the teachings of an ancient visionary named Abdul Alhazred.

Despite my passionate and determined course, I fear that in the end, I shall not succeed, so frighteningly fanatical and widespread, albeit secretive, are the influences of those Nameless Cults described in the work of Von Junzt. I even begin to worry that they've men on the faculties of Harvard and Miskatonic, and abroad, I'm afraid the mad ravings of an unhinged and disgraced American historian are not taken seriously. Then there were the copies Robert acquired and his work, which were never found.

But that there are copies in Argentina, France, and Great Britain (and those are just the ones I am able to confirm), information about Alhazred and his book in the New York Library, an unconfirmed and lost copy of the hideous grimoire in California are enough to confirm that these cults have spread beyond the borders of the Miskatonic River Valley—and indeed they did not even originate there. Then there is the fact that I believe the cultists are closing in on me despite my nomadic and largely anonymous existence since leaving Harvard and even Massachusetts behind me forever.

What I am here about to confess in detail, you will not find much information to corroborate, I fear. The cultists have done their work, and officially, it is the accepted position that Robert Phillips moved to Italy some three years ago, despite the absence of other evidence which would confirm that story to hold true. No missing persons report has been filed, and there is no further investigation into the case. In fact, there is no case at all.

Other vague references to cases of about a decade or so before this writing are confirmable to those who do research of their own. I would urge the reader to be careful in that research. If they must look further, the disappearances of a Massachusetts artist named Pickman[1], a man from Vermont named Akeley, many of the locals of a little-known town named Innsmouth (outside of the Miskatonic Valley), and a sinister man named Whateley all will lend further credibility to my tale.

That said, I beg you not to discredit Robert's story, no matter how weird or seemingly impossible the implications. I swear by any sanity and dignity that I have left that the whole of it is completely true. I am still an historian above all things, and uncovering the truth is ever the principle value of mine.

At the very least, hold all judgment until the bitter end and all the facts are laid bare. Then, when you find yourself drawing your own conclusions, even should you find me to be completely mad, I implore you not to delve into hidden and darksome things. There are realities within this world which men should rightfully fear even the barest knowledge of, and if you find yourself presented with a translated copy of a book known as *Al-Azif* or *The Necronomicon*, I beg you not to crack open even the cover of the tome and throw it into the fire as soon as you are alone.

In truth, I myself have questioned if what I saw in the end was not a mere hallucination or some trick the

---

[1] *Richard Upton Pickman was a renowned Boston artist, well known for his macabre paintings and who inexplicably disappeared in 1926.*

lights played that night in the old Phillips Manor, yet I cannot, in good faith, ignore how disturbing and real the incident had been at the time, nor what it all but confirmed, not least based upon my experiences with Robert leading up to that horrible night and confirmed by the research I've done since.

Though, perhaps I get ahead of myself. It would be best to begin my tale with how and when I met Robert, for it will give you a point of reference for how the character of this man of such great potential changed and to give a clear and stark point of reference before the beginning of my good friend's slow spiral toward his undoing.

It may seem pedantic and trivial, but I wish to describe the full scope of my dealings with Robert. I will attempt to give no conjecture as to events save for my own feelings at the time. After all, I am an historian by trade, and I wish to give whoever you are who is reading this the barest facts of the case as they were.

Because of the nature of my relationship with Robert, I offer this manuscript in two parts. The first being firsthand accounts of my interactions with Robert whilst we were both students at Miskatonic University, much written from memory, though a few scenes are directly quoted from the journals I kept between 1931 and 1936, each account written at or about the time of the incidents (and which, as of this writing, I still have in my possession)[2].

---

[2] *These journals were never found and were not among the papers of Professor Lewis, else select readings might have been appended to this text.*

The second half is largely made up of correspondences with Robert, with very few encounters. Where a complete letter is referenced (all twenty-two of them included with this manuscript, and in ascending order of their dates), I will refer to them by the dates on which Robert wrote them and the numbers which I have added to them that they might more easily be referenced and kept in a certain order.[3] I have no carbon copies of my own letters to Robert.

That said, let us begin.

*JAL*

---

[3] *Because of the nature of this publication and for the ease of the reader, the editor has included the letters from Robert Phillips directly in the pages at the point of Professor J. Lewis's references and removed Lewis's written references to the letters' numbers and dates. As for Prof. Lewis's own letters to Mr. Phillips, any attempt to locate them has come up empty, and the publisher can only surmise, like the journals (see note 2), they are unrecoverable.*

# ABOUT THE AUTHOR

J. M. DeSantis was born Jeffrey Michael DeSantis in New Jersey, USA. He is a writer and artist (Write-ist™) and the creator of the dark fantasy comic series, *Chadhiyana*™. Chiefly working in the genres of fantasy, horror, and humour, JMD has authored of a number of short stories, books, comics, and artworks. His work has appeared in print, digital publications, and even film around the world.

VISIT

# darkfirepress.com

FOR MORE CONTENT BY THIS
AND OTHER CREATORS

BOOKS + COMICS + CHILDREN'S BOOKS + ART
BOOKS & MORE

DARK FIRE PRESS™
Creator-Owned Publishing

www.ingramcontent.com/pod-product-compliance
Lightning Source LLC
Chambersburg PA
CBHW032220190726
48289CB00007BA/2322